PRAISE FOR SCENES FROM THE

Scenes from the Heartland is an unf̶_ ̶_ ̶_ ̶_ ̶_ ̶_ ̶_ ̶_ ̶_ ̶_ ̶_, ̶_ ̶_ ̶_ ̶_ ̶_ as it is honest, refusing to sentimentalize, transcending nostalgia, and looking directly at the riven, triumphant, glorious hearts of its characters. Donna Baier Stein provides a necessary reminder of everything we share, no matter how distant we may be in time or place."
—Lee Martin, Pulitzer Prize Finalist Author of *The Bright Forever*

In this gorgeous collection, Donna Baier Stein teases out the depth and humanity hinted at in Hart's two dimensional art, using each lithograph as a portal into a vivid, fully fleshed out world. Scenes from the Heartland is brimming with marvelous, generous scenes that truly do come from the heart.
—Gayle Brandeis, *The Art of Misdiagnosis*

Inspired by nine iconic lithographs, Donna Baier Stein indelibly imagines the forgotten lives of rural men and women in the early, backbreaking decades of the Twentieth Century. These stories of hardship and survival, of passions simmering under a roughshod surface, of alcohol-fueled cruelties and simple acts of kindness, both capture an era and transcend it. Scenes from the heartland, indeed.
—Dawn Raffel, *The Strange Case of Dr. Couney*

If Thomas Hart Benton's artwork could talk, I believe it would sound like Donna Baier Stein's prose—plainspoken, vivid, generous, and honest. The nine stories in this collection—which use Benton's lithographs as imaginative springboards—form a vibrant patchwork quilt of small towns, county fairs, and rural dance halls peopled by fiddlers and farmers, gas jockeys and traveling preachers. To read this book is to be transported, by Baier Stein's masterful storytelling, to the American heartland of a bygone era. I, for one, did not want to leave.
—Will Allison, *What You Have Left* and *Long Drive Home*

BOOKS BY DONNA BAIER STEIN

The Silver Baron's Wife
Sympathetic People
Sometimes You Sense the Difference
Letting Rain Have Its Say

Praise for The Silver Baron's Wife

An artistic, sympathetic imagining of the life of a 19th-century woman who made headlines for all the wrong reasons.
   —*Kirkus Reviews*

In this eloquent novel, Stein portrays the independent, eccentric, and resilient woman known as Baby Doe, a legendary figure from Colorado's silver boom. ... Stein's blend of love story, scandal, and mystical experience is satisfying and entertaining.
   —*Publishers Weekly*

A unique portrait of a time and place populated by fearless people, this reimagination of an uncommon woman is powerful.
   —*Foreword Reviews*

At long last we get to hear Baby Doe's compelling side of the hurtful tale that made her the most hated woman in the West. Donna Baier Stein has captured young Lizzie's Doe's agency in her first marriage, as well as older Lizzie's Tabor's deep spiritual resilience during her decades of isolation. Through Stein's artistry, Baby Doe's story makes the heart ache.
   —Judy Nolte Temple, *Baby Doe Tabor: Madwoman in the Cabin*

With T*he Silver Baron's Wife*, Donna Baier Stein pulls off that most difficult of novelistic feats: breathing fictional life into historic characters and situations. From the dark, unpropitious, and dismal depths of Baby Doe Tabor's biography, she mines a vein of pure silver.
   —Peter Selgin, *The Inventors*

Donna Baier Stein paints a heartfelt, poignant picture filled with loving details of Baby Doe's celebrated life that lingers long after the last page is turned.
   —Ann Parker, T*he Silver Rush Mystery Series*

Explosive, gripping and romantic ... An absorbing read about a fiercely independent woman who charted her own course only to find herself paying the price.
    —Talia Carner, *Hotel Moscow*

With sumptuous, tactile prose, rich historical detail, and an evocative recreation of the American West, *The Silver Baron's Wife* excavates the legend of Elizabeth McCourt Tabor to expose a character's humanity and soul.
    —Diane Bonavist, *The Cathars*

PRAISE FOR SYMPATHETIC PEOPLE

Donna Baier Stein is a discovery. Her deceptively mild story-telling veers swiftly into the savage but often unacknowledged discontent of suburban life—wives struggling with marital disappointment and missed opportunities, celebrating and often betrayed by unexpected friendships—all explored with language that engages and surprises.
    —C. Michael Curtis, *Fiction Editor, The Atlantic*

Ms. Baier Stein's stories are powerful in both language and character ... she balances a fierce wish to love and be loved with the hard reality of loss and failure, yet the yearning does not diminish. A profound accomplishment.
    —Elizabeth Cox, *The Slow Moon* and *The Ragged Way People Fall Out of Love*

Donna Baier Stein uncovers the sometimes heady glint of danger in relationships in a brilliantly edgy collection of stories that gets under your skin as even as it illuminates love, lust—and everything in between.
    —Caroline Leavitt, *New York Times bestselling author of Pictures of You and Is This Tomorrow*

Donna Baier Stein writes with the grace and precision of a poet ... here is a writer who trusts not only herself, but her readers, who will be skillfully guided into coming to their own satisfying conclusions.
    —Elizabeth Berg, *New York Times* bestselling author, most recently of *Tapestry of Fortunes*

SCENES FROM THE HEARTLAND

Stories Based on Lithographs by Thomas Hart Benton

by

Donna Baier Stein

Serving House Books

Scenes from the Heartland:
Stories Based on Lithographs by Thomas Hart Benton

Copyright © 2019 Donna Baier Stein

ISBN: 978-1-947175-10-5

Cover design by Tom Schneider / http://www.tomschneiderarts.com/

Front cover photo: "I Got a Gal on Sourwood Mountain" 1938 Lithograph, National Gallery of Art, © Benton Testamentary Trusts/UMB Bank Trustee/VAGA at Artists Rights Society (ARS), NY

Author photo by Denise Winters

Serving House Books logo by Barry Lereng Wilmont

Published by Serving House Books
Copenhagen, Denmark and Florham Park, NJ
www.servinghousebooks.com

Member of The Independent Book Publishers Association

First Serving House Books Edition 2019

Dedicated to my parents,
Martin and Dorothy Baier,
who gifted me with
Benton's "Spring Tryout"
and much more

CONTENTS

"Achelous and Hercules" by Thomas Hart Benton

MISSOURI AND MYTHICITY

Preface to *Scenes from the Heartland:*
Stories Based on Lithographs
by Thomas Hart Benton

Thomas Hart Benton (1889-1975) had deep roots in Missouri —his great-great uncle and namesake was the United States senator for whom every county in the state seems to name a school. Indeed, the Benton family was inseparable from that mythic age when Missouri came into the union. Of course, Missouri is in the middle of everything, in every sense. Its citizens think of themselves as northerners, easterners, westerners, southerners; (dialectologists affirm that each of those speech forms is well represented). It is rural, but St. Louis is among the most European (and oldest) of American cities. Politically, it's plum-colored. It grows corn; it grows cotton. It seceded during the Civil War—but not successfully, and it remained with the North. It is iconic river country, and yet its Ozark mountains and western prairies are equally emblematic. And this is the point: it is all regions, and none specifically. To be a Missourian is to contain multitudes. Like LaMancha, it is at once the least mythic of places, and the most perfectly so.

Another famous child of that dreamtime made his little river village into Everyone's Hometown, and his child self into Every

Boy (a mytheme long past its sell-by date, but compelling in its day). Twain actually decamped in late adolescence, scarcely so much as visiting again in his long life, and the same was true of Benton. But those geniuses remained the offspring and agents of that realm suspended in time and space. Who could say in what year or off what freeway exit you could find Tom Sawyer's "white town drowsing in the sunshine of a summer's morning"? Nor could you put a timestamp on "Achelous and Hercules." The enormous canvas, 22 feet long, 5 feet wide, deploys Benton's signature technique—call it a vision— of impossibly fluid human figures who seem independent of gravity, borne on unseen currents, and engaged in balletic struggle against primeval forces, to an effect that is at once realistic and kabuki-like. It is a Greek myth playing itself out in an utterly ordinary Missouri harvest-time. It is prosaic and poetic, thoroughly present and transcendently timeless.

While no painter can be without influences, and none so famous could be totally without effects on a further generation, Benton had no recognized forbears (though many have sensed a kinship to El Greco), and he had students, but no epigoni. There have been weak attempts to assign him to a Regionalist school, or to associate him with a fleeting fashion for identifying painting with music (if you ask me, some of David Inshaw's canvases capture a similar glimpse of eternities). But look at a photo of him: he was an angular figure whose clothes never quite fit. He was the sort of interpreter who awaits an interpretation, and so here you have the stories of Donna Baier Stein.

These stories do not merely invert the usual relationship between text and illustration, but offer a concrete *now* to which such a timeless glyph as "Edge of Town" might relate. She is deft but restrained with the period details that rough in a context without limiting its possibilities. It's like the bluejeans and fedora of the heroic figures in "Achelous and Hercules" that tell us this is a primal conflict, ancient before the ancients, but it is also the autumn of 1947, not far from Neosho, Missouri. Baier Stein observes her characters and their surroundings with similar precision. She knows something about growing corn, about foaling, about fiddles. She's heard of bonesetters (the folk-medical forerunners of osteopathy, also a product of Missouri). Deploying such minutiae is a technique for lending authority and concreteness, but it also feels like a reassurance of good faith, that these people *matter*.

They are distillations, or maybe avatars of a recognizable type, never caricatures. Few artists or writers can long ride that fenceline without fouling it (for example: Rockwell is now increasingly recognized as an artist of some seriousness, but he often made that mistake). For the artist, whether she works in pigment or pixels, real respect for human beings, as such, requires unflinching acknowledgement of their complexities and contradictions. Otherwise they decay into mere allegorical tropes (that is another error Benton continually threatens to commit—yet never does). In "A Landing Called Compromise," Baier Stein represents cattiness and charity as equal psychic pillars. Neither is offered as the *true* nature of the community or its people; the bringing of food to the church is at once an act of communion and a gesture of dominance. These people are relentlessly petty, with very little self-understanding—but the same is quite as true of their generosity. It is precisely through this, only through this, that the sacramental nature of the representation comes through: the characters are agents of something that transcends themselves, their time. They are bigger than themselves, and do not know it. They hear of movements of armies in distant places—Germany, Russia, Poland—without quite knowing where those places are. Similarly, in "Spring 1933" (both the story and the stardate) nobody knows that a way of life is definitively ending, that terrible things are in the offing. This is a point of mature craft: good writers know that dread—fear of the known and inevitable—is truer to our lived lives and harder for the writer to manage than suspense, the fear of the unknown.

The story, like the others, plays out on broad surfaces—field, sky —and in stark particulars: hat, ham, horse. It is the literary analogue to Benton's stringing of loosejointed, scarecrow-like figures along that merciless clothesline where earth and sky abut. Baier Stein, like Benton, gives tactile details: the grit of earth, the slime of chicken guts. The tales, like the paintings, say "this is a real and specific time, place. In fact, it is much more real than any particular time and place." "Trouble at the Dance Hall" (which *GHLL* had the honor first to publish) floats figures in defined space as Dante put Paolo and Francesca before us, buffeted about on the wind of their own passion. They are people whose human tragedy leads the poet to faint, and they are also just two more of an endless parade of untargeted souls who had desires, and constraints, lived in the moment, saw nothing beyond it, made choices, and suffered consequences.

There is another sense in which myth and concrete reality fade into one another with these images and these stories. The world of Benton's pictures and of Baier Stein's narratives is at the edge of living memory. The Blalocks do not know that what they are living through is the Flood of 1937. My own elders told me about that cataclysm. This spring, I buried my father, who knew that world well. It is now only knowable from the storytellers. My dad might well have written this, about his grandfather, who was indeed tall, gangly, rubber-jointed (it is an actual physical type of the region) and pastor of a succession of such Ozarks churches:

> "Look out then at the darkening sky!" the preacher thundered. Helen looked up to see him standing now at the pulpit, arm bent at one bony elbow, fingers outstretched, long fingers and a surprisingly short thumb, the fingers pointing east, away from the last light of the day still pouring through the open window.

The world is outside us, indifferent, overwhelming. And yet we are us and we are here. There are indeed human interiors, that matter, and yet do not:

> It was like there were two levels to living, Helen thought. The one where the fields got plowed and cows were bred. And the one underneath no one talked about, where folks needed care.

> "Who seeth us? And who knoweth us?" the preacher was asking, each word drawn out long like his arms and fingers, and said with such intensity Helen almost expected the letters themselves to hang in the air before his open mouth.

In the face of unimaginably vast forces that will have very specific and personal effects—the incomprehensible world war that is chugging inexorably nearer, in the form of the train that will take her son from her—a woman resorts to pellucid memory of a trifling event six years earlier:

> We'd taken a streetcar, green with yellow lettering on its side. Number 33. We'd walked past the reflecting pool at the entrance, stared up at the fifty-foot-high glass conservatory. Inside, we'd walked around the concrete balcony, looking up and down on all the living things: hundreds of flowers, plants, and trees, all of them lit by sunshine streaming in through thousands of panes of glass set in verdigris wrought-iron supports. Hundreds of chrysanthemums in a formal Chinese design. Trees stretching toward the art deco roof. Baskets of flowering plants hanging from the ceiling. Roses growing up forest-green trellises, tall stalks of iris, even an orange tree growing like a miracle indoors.

In case anybody ever asks you what William Carlos Williams meant by saying so much depends on a red wheelbarrow glazed with rain water beside the white chickens? *That.*

Enjoy. We often say that a given writer has finally found the proper illustrator—Tenniel for *Alice in Wonderland*, Cruikshank for Dickens. Here, the pictures found their storyteller.

Adam Brooke Davis
Truman State University

"Flood" by Thomas Hart Benton

A Landing Called
Compromise

The winter of '37 was the worst folks living in the bootheel had ever seen. Most days brought rain, snow, sleet, or an ominous mix of the three. On Friday, February 24, rain skated down in silvered sheets, painting long, watery tails on the tall windows of the one-room schoolhouse where Martha Blalock had taught for thirty years.

She eyed the class, tallying the small heads to make certain all her children were properly seated, hands folded on their desks, before dismissal. She ran a tight ship, yet the students loved her.

"Mrs. Blalock?" Gloria Hendry twisted the end of one braid, the color of butter-and-sugar corn.

Martha pushed her new plastic horned-rim glasses up her nose. She'd self-prescribed by trying on various pairs at the department store up in Caruthersville, saving the expense of a three-dollar visit to the eye doctor. Everything still seemed slightly out of focus.

"Yes, dear, what is it?" she asked.

"We're s'posed to go to church after school," Gloria said in that self-righteous whine Martha hated. "And I don't want to go out in this rain."

Other heads bobbed up and down: Hollins Carter, Betty James, Ronnie Hinote, more.

"My Pa told me to walk, even in the rain," Ronnie said. He was a scrawny boy, poorly tended to since his mother died last year.

"All of you are going to the church then?" Martha asked, wondering if this was something the new minister had set up. Poor fellow, sent to New Madrid Baptist just two weeks earlier, after the last interim pastor had left. Martha feared that this new one, the Reverend Elijah Berry, was out of his depth, having no inkling of the tumultuous history of the church.

She'd been meaning to set up a meeting with Reverend Berry, to show him the lay of the land so to speak, but this everlasting rain had delayed her. She wondered if a Pastor-Church Covenant had even been written to clarify expectations. One good thing about the Baptist church: if a congregation didn't like their pastor, they could always fire him.

Still, that thought was presumptuous at this point. The poor man had just started, for goodness' sake, and if he'd been listening to the wrong folks, he might well have gotten the wrong idea about how things were run.

"You're supposed to go to church this afternoon? In all this rain?" Martha asked, still skeptical.

More nods swept through the room.

"What on earth for?" A flush warmed her cheeks. Heaven forbid the children think she didn't want them going to church. She'd been a loyal member of the New Madrid Baptist Church since her own childhood and felt suddenly ashamed she'd let a nuisance like the weather keep her from services these past two weeks.

Gloria released her braid to wave her hand in the air. "For the Good News Club," she burst out before Martha had given her permission to speak.

"The Good News Club?" Martha repeated. "What's that?" She looked beyond Gloria's head, toward the colorful pictures of Bible stories torn from old issues of the *Concordia* that lined the back wall. There was Jesus The Shepherd Carrying A Lamb, Peter Denying His Savior, The Romans Laying Hands On Jesus, and Our Saviour Beginning His Suffering. Martha had bought the leaflets when her son, Gene, was three and shown them to him so often the pages were worn almost translucent. When Gene left home to join the Coast Guard, her husband Carl asked her to throw out all those back issues taking up space in the attic. Instead, she simply moved them behind an old unusable pie cabinet that tilted due to a missing leg. She would throw out a few issues, she reassured Carl, but saved their covers to tape to her classroom wall. They reminded her of those long-ago days when Gene was a little boy and she and Carl so blessedly young themselves.

"Yes, ma'am," Ronny Hinote said. "We're s'posed to go to church now every Wednesday after school. Mrs. Blix will be mad if we aren't there on time."

Gloria nodded her head.

Martha's ears pounded, and her vision clouded even more. Reverend Berry must have announced this new club on Sunday, in her absence. "Mrs. Zula Blix?" she asked slowly, being careful not to let her voice betray her anger.

"Yes, ma'am." Ronny wrapped a leather strap around his books and threw it over his shoulder. When Martha didn't reprimand him, the room grew noisy as the other children also gathered up their pencils, books, and canvas lunch totes.

"I will drive those of you going to the church myself," Martha said, shouting over a rolling drum of thunder from outside as she quickly took control of the situation.

Somehow, all nine children fit into the Ford woody wagon, and they made their way through bucketing rain to the church. She drove at a snail's pace on the dirt roads, especially through the dark puddles, ever mindful of how quickly accidents can happen and how precious the little ones in her charge were.

"You will not believe who they asked to teach my students Bible stories after school," Martha said that night as she lay in bed with Carl. Without waiting for an answer, she said, "That she-devil Zula Blix herself. What on earth is this world coming to?"

Carl cleared his throat then wrapped his hairy arms around her angular frame. "Now, Martha," he began.

"You know what that woman is like. What that entire family is like. Not a one of them should be teaching this town's children the Word of the Lord. 'Specially not Zula." Martha sighed loudly.

She had already decided to speak to the new Reverend Elijah Berry about his responsibilities to the church, what he was expected to do, and what he was not. A Child Evangelism Program was all well and good, she would say, but it required the proper teacher. She would offer herself as its head. Though she knew gossip was a sin, sometimes one simply had to do it. The Blix family had a long history of flouting at least three of the Lord's Commandments. The new Reverend should know; the children of New Madrid deserved no less.

"Why, she's not even from Missouri!" Martha's bad eye started twitching, and she turned to face her husband. "Carl," she whispered. "I can't stand to see Zula contaminate the minds of my children."

Carl patted her shoulder uncomfortably, as if that would help. He had reassured her multiple times there had never been a spit of anything between him and Zula after her rich husband died last year. But Martha had seen the widow flirt with every man in the congregation, whether they were married or not and no matter what side of the aisle they sat on.

The New Madrid Baptist Church had been built on a half-acre clearing in the woods high on a hill inside the oxbow curve of the Mississippi River, on the state line at a landing called Compromise. New Madrid County, Missouri, sat on one side and Fulton County, Kentucky, on the other. Half the church's thirty benches of hand-hewn sycamore were in one state and half in the other, enabling the members of the congregation to walk up the aisle on their side of the church and attend services without ever stepping into the other state. Come Sundays, folks would file in, lean their guns against the wall, and sit down in the pews on their designated side. Everyone would kneel for prayer except a man who stood guard at the end of each aisle in case any member from the opposite pews decided to start a fight. No one had caused any trouble for ages, but the guns were still kept at the ready. Families from the two counties had been feuding since the Civil War, when a flag officer from Fulton County turned traitor and helped a Union gunboat attack Island Number 10, leading to the Confederates' first loss of a battle position on the Mississippi.

Martha Blalock's kin lived in New Madrid County. Zula Blix and her folks lived in Fulton County. But even beyond the historic feud, Martha had harbored an extra helping of hate toward Zula and her kin ever since the woman had shown up for Sunday services mere months after her husband died, wearing a jade and teal dress with flared skirt and low scooped neck. Zula had blinked her eyelashes and touched the sleeve of every man she saw. Carl hadn't responded, but Martha had distrusted the woman ever since. Martha enjoyed criticizing Zula not to her face, but to her husband and her cousin Beulah every chance she got. Still, no matter how often Carl and Beulah agreed that yes, it was far from encouraging that Zula came from a suspiciously wealthy, drinking, firearm-toting Kentucky family and even worse that her oldest boy had gotten away with what he did all those years ago, Martha still sometimes doubted her superiority over the other woman. And her stomach sometimes twisted when

Zula wore a pretty, certainly expensive dress to church or drove through town in her fancy new red-and-black Chevy coupe.

Next to her in bed, Carl grunted.

But Martha wasn't finished. "I'll start making phone calls in the morning. Get the ladies from church on my side so we can approach the Reverend together. I'll have a few over for coffee so we can figure out the best way to remove Zula from her teaching duties in this new program. Why, the woman never even attended church while her husband was alive."

"You hate having folks to the house," Carl said, expertly reaching through the moonlit dark to touch the lid of her right eye, closing it because that sometimes stopped the twitch.

Martha considered the long cane she'd propped against the wall before climbing into bed, wondering if she should get up now and thumb through her mother's cookbook for a coffee cake recipe. "I hear Zula's always having folks over for fancy teas and card games. Even folks from our side of the river. If you can imagine! So I've got to make it clear mighty fast that I'd do a much better job getting the Lord's Word into the ears of our children before it's too late. A much better job."

Carl patted her bony shoulder. "Time for shut-eye, Martha May. You know I've got work tomorrow."

She turned away from him, careful not to put any weight on her bad hip. At least her eye had stopped its spasms. They'd been worse this week, and Martha feared it might be the new glasses. "But the weather's so bad," she said, knowing he'd still be up before dawn to deliver the county's mail the next morning.

He turned away from her but spoke softly over his shoulder, "You'd be a fine teacher at the church."

Carl got weather reports and most of his news from the ham radio he'd built from a kit sold by the Wholesale Radio Company. He'd run a long wire antenna across the backyard from the house and stretched it to a pole. Now he could pick up stations from all over the world. On the day of President Roosevelt's second inauguration, he and Martha had sat in ladderback chairs next to each other, holding hands, listening. Martha liked picturing this important scene taking place so far away from them, and she liked the excitement in the announcer's voice as he described the abnormally terrible weather there in Washington, D.C. A half inch of rain had drenched the floor of the President's open car! This winter was definitely the wettest and coldest Martha had ever lived through, and yesterday a radio operator had reported the river was still rising unusually fast and had nearly reached the door of the Piggly Wiggly over in Paycock.

Months later, in June, Carl would tell her a story he'd heard about a girl listening to her family's shortwave one afternoon. "She was sitting on the floor," Carl would say, "turning the dial to see if she could pick up something interesting when she heard a woman's voice. The woman sounded upset. 'This is Amelia Earhart. This is Amelia Earhart,' the voice repeated. Over and over. The girl tried to take notes, but the signal kept fading. She heard the woman speak to a man, who sounded delirious. They were in an airplane, on land, but 'the water was rising.'" Carl's eyebrows raised high. "Imagine that," he would say as they sat on the front porch looking out across their finally dry field. "A little girl, God knows where, is able to hear the voice of one of the most famous people in the world. God knows where Amelia Earhart was, too, of course. But we are mighty, mighty fortunate to have the miracle of ham radio in our lives."

Martha wasn't as excited by this anecdote as Carl was. It seemed to her that the ham radio had done no one any good in that instance. Knowing someone needed help and being able to give it were two very different things. The girl had, after all, not saved Amelia Earhart. She wondered if the girl might even grow up to be haunted by that fact.

Rain still fell the day after Martha decided to oust Zula Blix from her teaching position at the new and poorly considered Good News Club. As soon as she'd fed Carl cream toast and broiled ham and sent him off to the post office, she wiped her hands on her red gingham apron, lifted the receiver on the Bakelite wall phone, and put in a call to her cousin Beulah.

"I'm going to invite some ladies from church over for coffee. Soon as this rain stops. We need to discuss the new Reverend. And Zula Blix."

"Hush!" Beulah shouted. Her dog Oleo stopped barking in the background. Then, more directly to Martha, "What's Zula done now?"

Martha cleared her throat. "Seems the new pastor took it in mind to start a Good News Club last week. This in addition to regular Sunday School classes!"

"I only met the man first time last week at church. Seems a self-satisfied sort," Beulah said. "Pudgy, as though he won't mind any of the desserts we ladies bring to socials. I heard he came to us from Mount Horeb. You were there for the vote, weren't you, Martha?"

Martha twisted the cord connecting the receiver. "Yes, yes. It's not Reverend Berry I want to talk about though it does appear he started this problem."

"I miss Reverend Hunnycutt," Beulah said, her voice low. "Made me no nevermind that he was just an itinerant preacher. It just felt good every time he passed through New Madrid. So what's this Good News you mentioned?"

"All my students are in it," Martha answered. "Just heard about it yesterday from that sweet, though spoiled, little Gloria. She told me that she and all my other students were supposed to head to church soon as school ended. That there was a new club, and it was under the tutelage of Mrs. Zula Blix. If you can imagine."

"Well, I can tell you that last Sunday Miss High and Mighty seemed to have our new preacher wrapped around her little finger. I'm wondering if she offered him some money from her husband's estate. I'm still not sure why she suddenly decided to be a church-goer!"

"To find a new man obviously," Martha said. She paused, wondering how many of the teacups on the green painted shelf next to the sink were chipped.

"If the new reverend takes money from her, they'll probably

claim the whole church building lies in Kentucky or even move it so it doesn't straddle state and county lines."

Martha felt flushed with anger and took three breaths like Carl had taught her.

"You still on the line?" Beulah asked.

"I'm here. I don't plan to hold back when a group of us goes to speak to the Reverend. He needs to know the stained history of that family. All of it." The words were spitting out of her at a too-fast pace. "Good News indeed! I bet she'll let the boys in that club run outside 'stead of sitting and memorizing Bible verses like they ought to!"

"Maybe it's best to give Zula a few weeks to get herself into her own hot water," Beulah said, and Zula nodded as though Beulah could see her full agreement through the phone line even if she had no intention of waiting for anything other than this rain to stop.

Martha reached for her purse on the Formica counter and rummaged through it, trying to find that memo book with the pretty blue hollyhocks on its cover. She'd remembered she needed to add lard to her grocery list so she could make Gene's favorite pie.

"How's Willie doing?" she asked. "Gene's comin' home for a short leave, and I know he'll want to see his favorite cousin."

Beulah's son had been paralyzed twenty years earlier, in an accident when Gene, and Willie, and Ralph Blix had gone swimming at the Landing.

"Willie's gonna be glad to hear that," Beulah said. "He's got some shooting pains in his right leg. Never understood how his legs can hurt like that. But he claims they burn when it rains."

"I'm sorry to hear that. You give my nephew a special kiss from me. And tell him Gene's coming," Martha said.

Inside the clutch, Martha found her handkerchief, the picture of Jesus on gold foil she never went anywhere without, a comb missing a few teeth, and finally the memo book. She took a deep breath again to calm herself. "You go to prayer meeting Tuesday night?" she asked her cousin.

"Mmm-hhhm," Beulah said. "Zula was there in all her finery, of course. Fancy plaid rain slicker, matching hat and umbrella. I swear that woman ought to spend more time on living the Word of the Lord than on her wardrobe."

"Amen," Martha said.

"I'm glad our boys got through their religious education long afore she was in charge," Beulah said.

Gene, and Beulah's boy, Willie, had been so sweet, both of them with their thick blond curls. They'd spent hours together down at the Compromise Landing, fishing, jumping off the pier in their dungarees, bare-chested and tan. Unfortunately, against her wishes, Gene and Willie had also taken a liking to Zula Blix's boy Ralph. She never knew how they'd met and tried to put an end to it, but somehow the three boys kept in touch and she knew, though Gene hadn't been the one to tell her, that even now as young men they still went into town to shoot a game of pool whenever Gene was home on leave. Ralph Blix had been the fool who suggested they all jump off the pier at low tide that long-ago summer, but neither Gene nor cousin Willie seemed to hold a grudge, a fact Martha could not wrap her head around. These days, Gene always insisted on taking his cousin along whenever he went into town, pushing Willie in his wheelchair, sometimes standing on the back riding down the short hill at the top of Main Street, both boys, now grown men, whooping and hollering like they were ten. In Gene's last letter to Martha and Carl, he'd said he planned to take Willie out to find some pretty girls. In a postscript, he'd reminded his mother to make his favorite foods: noodles baked with tomato sauce, mushrooms, and bacon. Fried potato cakes. And that lemon meringue pie.

"Tell Pa to get the fishing waders ready, too," he'd added in his rushed handwriting. "He and I are due some bluegill."

Beulah coughed on the other end of the phone line. "You go down to see the river yesterday?" she asked, bringing Martha back to their call.

"Nope. Didn't step outside." Martha tucked the memo pad with her grocery list back into her purse. Gene would be home for a week. She'd have to tell him to steer clear of Ralph Blix. Just until this issue with the Good News Club was resolved. She couldn't have her own kin act disloyal.

Oleo barked again in the background. "Hush, you mutt!" Beulah said without a trace of anger in her voice. "I'm about to throw this sweet critter out into the rain. He's been cooped up all week and is driving me crazy."

Beulah huffed, and Martha pictured her cousin bending over to soothe the old dog. "What about the river?" Martha asked.

"It's bad, worst I've ever seen it," Beulah said. "Heard the levee over at Clear Creek went out. And they're evacuating Butler County."

"I swear I don't remember a February this bad. Of all times for us to get a new preacher." Martha ran her finger around the mouthpiece of the phone. It had been so much easier when she and Beulah were girls. She wasn't sure she liked being a grown-up much, all the responsibility that now fell on her shoulders to make sure the world ran the way she wanted it to run. "Amen," she said again for no reason, then, "Talk to you tomorrow."

But the next morning, phone lines were down in New Madrid. Scores of trees had fallen into the river, and temperatures had dropped 25 degrees overnight. Outside, sleet came down hard. Some of it stuck to the windowpanes, freezing on contact.

By Friday water came up to the edge of their yard. Carl went out to move their two cows to a small barn up on higher ground. He'd had to lead the animals carefully over the ice around the flooded areas.

Electricity was out, but Carl's ham radio still worked. The news was nonstop now, the voices on the radio increasingly frantic.

State in Grip of Ice as Cold Wave Rushes In
Poplar Bluff Flood Victims Vacate Homes
Indiana Village under 12 Feet of Water

Martha and Carl sat by the ham radio after dinner. At dusk, the door swung open, and their son blew in with a gust of icy wind. Gene, taller than his father now, was bundled in a hooded black rubber raincoat. Bits of ice clung to his dark beard.

"You're comin' with me," he said. "Everybody's meeting up at the church."

"Oh my goodness, Gene, you're home!" Martha cried. She ran toward him, forgetting her cane, and wrapped him, wet raincoat and all, in her arms. Her wildly beating heart settled into a deep calm inside her. Her beautiful boy, her love.

"Welcome home, son!" Carl had risen from his chair as well. "Didn't expect you getting in tonight. Planned to pick you up at the station tomorrow morning. Coast Guard let you off early?"

Gene answered over his mother's shoulder. "One of the guardsmen picked me and our petty officer up. This leave is going to be a working one."

Martha pulled back to better see his face. "What do you mean?"

"The floods. We've got search and rescue units out all over the state."

"I'd heard the president and Morgenthau were directing relief efforts," Carl said, avoiding his wife's eyes.

"And I'm part of it," Gene said, extricating himself from his mother's arms, smiling ruefully at her water-stained dress.

"But I made a pie." Martha blinked.

Gene eyed the room. "I've got to get you two up to safety."

"I'm not leaving this radio, son," Carl said. "Your mother and I'll be fine long as we stay indoors. Come give your old Pa a hug then pull up a chair. We've lived through rains before."

"Not like this one." Gene pulled coats and hats from hooks near the door.

"Get out of those wet clothes, Gene," Martha said quietly. "I'll get dinner ready. Listen to your Pa."

"No," Gene said firmly. Martha hardly recognized her son's voice, that of a man now. "You have to come with me. Both of you. Fella's got a radio set up at church. And my petty officer wrangled a wagon to pick up stragglers. We already rounded up folks from Paycock, and I persuaded him to drive over here for you. We've got no time to waste, Ma. They're waiting outside."

When she didn't answer, he said, "You say you've got food?"

He looked toward the kitchen and catching sight of the pie Martha had baked that afternoon, he strode in quickly, dipped his finger into the browned meringue. His eyes sparkled when he turned to grin at her in that old way of his.

But his face grew serious quickly, the way it had when he told her how Willie's pup Blackie had swum around in circles that day they all jumped off the pier and Willie didn't come up when they expected him to. "That dog was trying to tell me something. I wouldn't have known Willie was hurt if the pup hadn't done that." It was Gene who dived down and dragged his unconscious cousin back to shore.

Martha shuddered.

"Let's pack up this pie," Gene said. "Come on now."

Martha walked into the kitchen as though in a dream. Without saying another word, she covered the Pyrex pie plate with its ruby red lid, then let Gene help her into her coat.

"Why not take the car?" Carl asked.

"Can't risk getting water in the engine," Gene said. "And we're already loaded up here on the wagon, both folks and supplies."

Carl kept asking questions, but Gene said he'd explain everything later.

It was sleeting so hard when Gene took them outside, Martha could barely make out the open bed wagon sitting there, its wheels slick with mud. Gene helped her up into a seat on the side and placed the pie plate gently on her lap. Then he bent down and kissed the top of her head. She was shaking but grasped the plate tightly. Carl took an empty seat next to her, and she was thankful for the feel of him against her thigh. Two men sat across from them on another bench, both in dark green raincoats and rubberized hats.

"Heard they found a girl with a newborn baby on her lap," one said to the other. "Both of 'em frozen on the roof over in Sikeston."

Martha's eye started twitching like mad. She tried to reach for Carl's hand, get his calm reassurance that they'd all be back in their houses in the morning, but he had turned to the young man next to him.

"I'm Darryl. Honored to serve with your son, Mr. Blalock."

Carl nodded, looking proud.

"Roosevelt's sending in the WPA as well as the Coast Guard," Darryl said.

"Where's Gene gone?" Martha asked.

"Up there." Darryl pointed toward the buckboard.

The sleet was hitting Martha's face, and she put a hand over her eyes to try to see. There were two horses up front, their coats stained dark. One of them whinnied as a whip cracked on its back, but whatever words Gene might be shouting at them were lost in the wind as the wagon moved forward.

The pie plate sat on her lap, its lid slick with ice pellets. Martha bent protectively to cover it. When lightning flashed, she caught a glimpse of the land around them, covered in irregularly-shaped splotches of water, houses abandoned with no lights showing through their windows, farm tools and what she realized with a start must be small, dead livestock littering the fields.

They approached the church on one of two gravel roads that bordered the one-story frame building. The scene Martha half-stumbled into at the church was grim, the sanctuary packed with refugees from the flood. Six double-hung windows were all that kept them from the dark storm outside.

Still clutching her pie plate, Martha looked around the room. There was Gloria Hendry sitting with her parents on the wide plank floor in a back corner, fiddling as always with her braids, and Ronnie Hinote sat shivering alone nearby. Another young boy Martha didn't recognize held a rag to his forehead; when he removed it, it was soaked in blood. Everywhere, there were people needing to be helped. Some were folks she knew; others were strangers from across the state border. For the first time she could remember, the church wasn't cut in half down the middle of the center aisle. The pews had been pushed willy-nilly.

A woman sat with one baby on her lap and two little ones at her feet, all of them crying. They must have been from Fulton County because they didn't go to Martha's school.

When Gene and Carl went to join some men huddled near the pulpit, Martha found Ronnie Hinote. "It'll be fine," she told him. "You'll see."

The boy sniffed and wiped his nose on the sleeve of his corduroy shirt before Martha could stop him.

A garish Jesus had been installed behind the altar a month ago. His eyes bulged like he had gout. The monstrous gift had been donated by Zula Blix; for what ulterior motive, Martha didn't know. But she didn't like it; this was *not* her Jesus.

Underneath the Blix-approved Jesus, Cousin Willie sat in his wheelchair wearing a plaid shurt. Gene had his hand on his shoulder. She could hear a familiar static from someone's ham radio.

"Carl," she called out. "Gene."

Carl turned and raised his hand in that usually reassuring way of his, meaning "Calm down now, I've got this." But it didn't help this time, and still holding her pie plate in one hand and the cane in the other, she took a step back to brace herself against the paneled wall and get her bearings.

The Reverend Elijah Berry also stood up at the front of the church near the Excelsior Stove and an urn of coffee. His cheeks were flushed, and his forehead sweaty. His arms akimbo, like a feudal lord surveying his kingdom, Martha thought. She couldn't stand the little she'd seen of the man. He was obsequious, overly attentive, sprinkling too many extravagant adjectives into his speech and sermons. He made her want to shower after church, and yet she regularly went, reminding herself that the real wisdom of the Lord came from inside, that the red-cheeked buffoon standing behind the pine altar could display all the gaudy crucifixions of Jesus he liked, she herself would not be fooled. He paid more attention to the rich than the poor, badmouthed parishioners behind their back, oozed charm if he thought it would benefit himself then just as suddenly withdrew it.

She bit her lip, remembering her desire to replace Zula Blix as head of the child evangelism program. She'd have to ooze out some charm of her own as well. Remembering what Beulah had said about the Reverend's being partial to pies, she decided she'd bake one and take it to him next week. By then, surely the rain would have stopped.

The room was lit only by candles and kerosene lamps that cast both light and shadows. A long table had been pushed against the beaded wood wainscoting on the far wall. There were plates piled high with sandwiches and cookies, even a sliced ham. And there was Zula Blix, in some silly emerald green suit, standing at the end of the table, instructing people where to put their contributions.

Martha took three deep breaths, and then made her way carefully to the other end of the table where she put the pie plate down in front of the ham. When the lid was lifted, most of the meringue still stood in stiff glossy peaks, white with brown tips, just the way national champion pie-maker Monroe Strause suggested. "It isn't the pie but overeating that brings on that 'Great American tummy ache,'" he'd said on a radio show.

A carefully manicured index finger, painted in tangerine polish, appeared and pushed Martha's Pyrex dish back behind the ham.

"Desserts are kept in the back," whoever belonged to the finger said dismissively. Then Martha caught sight of the small hand's middle finger, with its large pearl and onyx ring.

"Zula Blix, take your hands off my pie!" she shouted, louder than she'd intended. Reverend Berry looked toward the two women, eyebrows raised, but Zula waved to him reassuringly, as if to say "Nothing I can't handle."

Martha pursed her lips.

"How are you, Martha?" Zula's voice oozed fake interest. "Isn't this an awful night?" She gave one more tap with that orange-polished nail, sliding the pie another quarter inch toward the wall. "Ralph's already been out once helping to find those left behind, the elderly and infirm and such." She nodded toward where her pale-faced son was warming up by the stove, talking to the Reverend, then she looked toward Willie. Gene was bent over, whispering into his cousin's ear, both hands on the arms of the wheelchair. "Your boy going to get out there, too?" Zula asked. "Or is the rain comin' down too hard now?"

Martha wanted to punch her. But Beulah appeared suddenly at her elbow. "Come on, Martha, let's go back to the menfolk."

Martha put both hands on the knob of her walking stick to hide their shaking. Zula Blix had no cause for such holier-than-thou talk.

But her cousin was right. Now wasn't the time to take on Zula.

When she looked up to give Zula one last evil eye, the woman had wandered back to what was properly her side of the church. Just then the Reverend yelled, "We've got another one!"

Martha turned to see two men rush through the door she'd come through minutes earlier. They carried a body between them. Its hands looked hard and pale.

"Oh my Lord!" Beulah cried out.

Martha refused to give in to tears but felt far too shaky to make her way back to her husband and son. "Get Carl up here," she whispered. "And Gene, Beulah. Please. I fear I'm going to faint."

Beulah grabbed a chair from the end of the food table and slid it behind Martha, nearly pushing her down into it.

A third man, tall and barrel-chested, burst into the sanctuary. Martha recognized his Coast Guard coat, double-breasted brown with a sheepskin storm collar. "We need ten men," the man shouted. "Twenty if you've got 'em. We're heading out to the levee to pile more sandbags."

Gene shot up from where he'd been half-kneeling in front of the radio and hurried over. He squeezed the man's arm in familiar greeting. Ralph Blix joined them, though Zula had tried to stop him.

A dozen men now circled the newcomer.

"How we going to get there?" Martha heard Gene ask, his voice so much deeper now than when he'd sung in this very room in the Sunday School choir so many years ago. Even then, the choir had divided straight down the middle—Fulton County children on one side, New Madrid County on the other.

"We've got a barge we'll take over. Big one." The man was panting. "Lots of cutters out there already. Patrol boats, you name it. We're saving life and property fast as we can, but we need more manpower."

Martha turned to find Carl; he still sat near the radio. She was thankful he was too old to go out with these young men and thankful that he knew it. Ronnie Hinote was staring at her. The poor boy was obviously petrified. She leaned her head back on the chair, squeezed her eyes shut so he wouldn't know that she was scared too. Once she was sure the tears wouldn't fall, she smiled reassuringly at Ronnie. She was remembering those *Concordia* covers on the wall, picturing Jesus carrying that sweet helpless little lamb.

Then before she knew it, Gene and Ralph and the tall stranger and other young men had disappeared. The church felt suddenly empty, as though all the life and energy had been sucked out of it. Carl was walking toward her, eyes locked on hers. Martha tightened her grip on her cane and bit her lip to keep from crying out to her son to come back.

Those left behind—the women and children and old and infirm like Beulah's boy Willie—stayed all night in the sanctuary while rain pounded on the tin roof. Beyond the darkened windows, the rain slashed in angled sheets. Wind howled down the chimney, an invisible intruder intent on chilling their bones. It would be even colder outside in all that wind and rain. All Martha could think about was her sweet boy, out there in all that bitter freeze and blackness and all that water. She realized too late that in the rush of leaving home she'd left her purse. No Jesus on gold tinfoil to hold between her fingers. So she forced herself to look up at the ugly painted crucifix behind the altar, the one Zula Blix had donated, the one with its garish paint and wide open eyes on Jesus, praying hard and silent and deep.

The news didn't reach them til the next afternoon.

They'd finished all the ham and sandwiches and cookies and cakes. On the long table, Martha's ruby red pie plate was empty except for a lolling dollop of meringue, which she put on two fingers, offering one to Ronnie and one to Gloria, who had spent much of the night with her parents near her and Carl. Gloria's hair had escaped its braids and hung in limp curls on either side of her face.

Reverend Berry was leading them in singing "Peace in the Valley," his alto booming loud over the half-empty room. Across the way, Zula Blix stood in a cluster of Fulton County women. Amazing, Martha thought, how they'd all managed to be well-dressed in the middle of the storm.

When the tall man in the double-breasted jacket once again appeared in the doorway, the singing abruptly stopped. This time, he didn't even step across the threshold into the sanctuary. He just stood in the open doorway, crossing his arms over his chest. Carl snoozed in a chair beside Martha, and she reached for his hand.

"The barge overturned," the man said quietly. "Sometime during the night. A hundred and twenty men are dead or missing. Rescue efforts are under way."

He'd brought lists, he continued, waving long sheets of white paper in front of him. Names of the men still missing. Names of the men whose bodies had been recovered. Names of the men who were safe and being cared for.

When no one spoke, not even the Reverend, the man let the hand holding the lists fall to his side, then walked slowly over to the table. Someone stood to push aside empty platters, including the pie plate, and the man laid three long sheets of paper down.

"Reverend?" someone asked. It was an old man Martha didn't recognize from the other side of the church. Dressed in worn overalls, with a tobacco stain dripping from one corner of his mouth. Those damn Fulton County ne'er-do-wells, she thought. That man probably hated my Daddy, and my Daddy hated him.

The Reverend ignored him, pushing his way to the table, spreading his arms as though sharing a feast.

"The names are here," he said in that stage-y voice Martha hated. As though it were any of his doing, she thought bitterly. Always trying to be the one in front. The people in the room, including the old man in overalls, waited as though there would be more to come, more explanation of this horrible tragedy that had befallen them. When they saw none would be forthcoming, those that could rushed to the table, pushing the Reverend and the tall man aside.

Carl's hand escaped hers, and she watched him hurry over along with the others. But when Martha rose from her chair she hobbled directly toward the door where the man in the storm collar had stood. She knew Beulah would come after her, but she had to get to the river, because that's where Gene had set out for, and she had to find her boy.

Outside, the sky still gray and cloudless. Her cane sunk into the wet ground as she made her way forward as quickly as she could. Her shoes were soon muddied, but she kept on, stepping down the stone-lined path, down the long hill.

When she reached the river bank, the muddy water rushed by faster than she could have imagined. She closed her bad eye, not even giving it a chance to start its crazy dance. Her glasses had fogged, but she could see two half-drowned houses with water up to a foot or two below their eaves, their chimneys stained dark. There were the tops of two gnarled trees, leafless, their branches like an old lady's, like her own, arthritic fingers. Roiling dark clouds arched above them, black, blacker the higher you looked.

"Remember when we were kids Grandpa told us the river ran backwards one year?" Beulah had appeared at her side.

"Sure do. During the earthquakes," Martha said quietly. "In '11 or '12. He claimed his boat went upstream for nearly a mile. Never knew whether to believe him or not."

As she spoke, she wondered what it would feel like to step into the river rushing past her. Just three steps forward. Then lift a foot over the low row of sandbags. Lift the other foot, using the cane for balance. Then once the hem of her skirt was soaked, and she could feel the way the water grabbed at her ankles and skirt and the way she wanted to sit down in it, she could unclench her hand from the cane. It would float past her downstream, buffeted and rocked. There was only so much support one could count on.

She remembered her grandfather's tale of the water running backwards. She tried to picture that, the river running backwards and time with it, bringing her Gene back to her, or at least giving her the chance to say goodbye, or even bringing back the boy he'd been, the young woman she'd been before Jesus had gouty eyes and women flirted with her husband, before things got so complicated she couldn't figure out who were the good guys and who were the bad.

She felt a hand on her shoulder and turned to see Beulah. "Come on now, Martha, let's get you back inside afore you catch your death."

Back in the church, Martha saw the man in the Coast Guard jacket now sat near the pulpit. Someone had wrapped him in two dark brown wool blankets. A cup of coffee sat steaming beside him.

Martha moved toward Carl, who still stood in the crowd at the table, bent over a list, his finger scrolling down rows of names. She'd been so foolish to not go to an eye doctor; she couldn't see well at all with these cheap things. "Which list is that?" she asked when she came up behind him, heart pounding. She touched the sides of his waist. He didn't answer.

She stood hip-to-hip with him now, holding her breath as he moved his finger down more names. She took her new glasses off, wiped them, and glanced across the way where she saw, as though at a long distance that had suddenly shortened, Zula Blix, standing all alone in her fine emerald suit, now mussed. Martha didn't know if she'd had a chance to read the list to find Ralph's name or not. Or what their sons' fates might be. But she caught Zula's eye squarely, nodding curtly in recognition of all they both had to lose.

"I Got a Gal on Sourwood Mountain" by Thomas Hart Benton

TROUBLE AT THE DANCE HALL

My true love is a blue-eyed daisy,
Hi-diddy-O-diddy-diddy-I-day
If I don't get her, I'll go crazy,
Hi-diddy-O-diddy-diddy-I-day

My true love a blue-eyed daisy. No siree, Rufus Corn thought as he short-bowed his fiddle. *My* true love was a strappin' gal with skin like coffee and eyes like golden raisins. Gone now three years. Rufus resettled himself on the four-legged stool, watching a young woman on the dance floor. Her eyes were blue like the song said, her hair blond and curled. But he felt no lust—not because of his age, nearing 70—but because neither he nor the establishment would allow it. In fact, were he not providing the music, Rufus would not even be allowed inside this dance hall on the outskirts of Pangburn, Arkansas.

Fiddling was Rufus' calling. Every Friday night he came to this one-story white clapboard building called The I. Here he fulfilled the task he believed God had given him. He performed on a fiddle he had fashioned himself. The neck, sides, and back plate were made of maple; the front of spruce. After he'd sawed and glued the wood, he used a carving gouge to shape the corners and edges. He still carried this fine tool, with its sharp metal shaft and round wooden handle, in his back pocket.

That night, the Fourth of July, a bigger crowd than usual had gathered at The I. The Civilian Conservation Corps started that year by President Roosevelt had done the town the favor of building a large concrete platform for shooting fireworks out near the swimming hole.

Rufus guessed that The I's gravel parking lot and long front porch with wooden benches and white columns would be among the best spots in town for viewing the show. He'd watched folks coming into the place early, while the sun still hung a good stretch above the horizon. Some walked; some came in open-back trucks; some rode horses they tied to a railing at the end of the porch.

As Rufus stood for a short break, Gilroy Tucker, Publisher and Editor of *The Pangburn Press*, parked a fancy new Model B Ford far to the side, where the hooves of skittish horses couldn't reach. The summer The I opened three years earlier, a Letter to the Editor written by a Seventh Day Adventist had appeared in the paper. The bartender had pinned the clipping to a tar-papered wall, circling in red ink this part of the letter:

Whatever you call it, we are worse than our neighbors in Heber for they keep their sins outside the city limit and now we are going to allow music and drinking and dancing right in the middle of town.

A lifelong resident of Pangburn's shantytown, Rufus had always known how narrow-minded his rich white neighbors were. He wanted to open their eyes, make them aware of what was happening not only in their town but in the rest of the world. He'd learned to read in his thirties using the children's Bible stories the Sunday school teacher at his Baptist church shared with him. He now admired Gilroy Tucker's editorials warning about Adolph Hitler and the terrible goings-on across the ocean in Germany. He knew that most folks in this down-country town preferred to ignore evil, pretending the sun always shone even when it did not. But evil had reared its head nearby, too: Just last month, a black laborer had been killed by farmworkers and someone had posted a sign over on Route 10 warning Negroes to be out of town by sundown.

Rufus' stomach clenched thinking how he had nowhere else to go, being a widower with no children to take him in. He had decided he would stay in his shack even if they had to burn it down around him. To settle himself, he turned his attention back to the music.

Hi-diddy-O-diddy-diddy-I-day.

As he played and sang, Rufus watched the blond woman still dancing in the middle of the room. He'd seen her here often, had heard her name: Maisie. She came to The I most Friday nights and was beautiful like a painting, though one he could never touch. She was married to a man named Bill Kleitsch who was missing half a leg from a threshing accident. Kleitsch walked with the aid of a snake-head cane and drank whiskey from a Mason jar. Maisie and Bill came to The I most every week, and most every week Maisie would dance with some stranger who'd wandered into town, a traveling salesman, usually, on his way to Little Rock. Only a stranger would dare to dance with Maisie when mean Bill Kleitsch sat nearby. But the couple must have had some sort of agreement because Bill never said a word, just sat there drinking, and Maisie danced with whatever stranger was available. Whoever that out-of-towner was, thin or fat, tall or short, he was sure to fall a little bit in love with the blond angel so radiant in this small dance hall in this small town in Arkansas. Rufus saw it happen every time, and he saw how much Maisie depended on these strangers' infatuations with her.

As Rufus came to the last stanza of "Sourwood Mountain," Maisie caught him staring. He knew what she saw when she regarded him: a wiry black-skinned man with a too-long neck, worn overalls, and creek-washed shirt. She turned away, back to the tall stranger who was her dance partner that night. Maisie and the out-of-towner moved to sit at a table far from Bill and his men friends, who huddled at the end of the bar drinking. The stranger's hair was parted straight down the middle, and he was so tall he had a hard time fitting himself into his chair. He'd had to lower his head when he came through the door. Rufus could tell that the stranger, like all the others before him, had fallen head over heels for Maisie.

Outside the door, which remained open, a setting sun perched on the horizon like half of an orange slice.

Rufus adjusted his hat and touched his bow stick to the steel strings again. He'd cut the bridge on his fiddle low enough that he could play all three strings at once. Running the stick across them, he started on "New Five Cents." He'd tuned the fiddle so low it sounded like he was playing below C, and his voice dripped the lyrics like slow molasses:

> I wisht I had a new five cents, wisht I had a dime,
> I wisht I had a new five cents, to give that gal of mine.

The dance floor was definitely more crowded than usual on account of the fireworks. Couples swung wildly to and fro as Rufus continued the set by swinging into a reel. Since Maisie still sat with the stranger, Rufus watched another woman he recognized, Augusta Sweet, dancing alone near the back wall. She too was a lifelong resident of Pangburn, and he knew she came from a long line of respected bonesetters. Many tales were told about the magic cures her father Aloysius, now deceased, had brought about through his laying on of hands. Aloysius claimed his gift was divinely inspired, brought about through faith in Christ. Watching Augusta dance without shame, Rufus wondered if her father had passed on his bonesetting techniques and other wisdom to Augusta and why no man had ever married her.

Rufus' bow raced across the strings, faster and faster. His foot tapped the floor, one leg moving up and down like a slender piston. Then he made a sudden switch to a Wee Bonnie Baker tune, taking great pleasure in his ability to control the crowd. Augusta's long black dress swirled around her ankles like dark churning water. A chimney lamp swung above her stern, sad face, and he was once again puzzled as to why she always danced alone. Unlike Maisie, Augusta Sweet had neither beau nor husband. She wasn't what most folks would call pretty, not like Maisie, but there was a steadiness, a presence in her the young blond woman sorely lacked. Maisie needed to pull a stranger's attention to her each night she came to The I; Augusta made it clear she didn't require anything from anyone.

Rufus reckoned his fiddle playing sounded more inspired than usual. He picked up the pace again and watched Augusta dance passionately in the corner, letting the music move into and around her in ways he suspected no man had ever done.

> *How you can love!*
> *Oh, Johnny! Oh, Johnny!*
> *Heavens above!*

The tall stranger grabbed Maisie up from her chair, pulling her onto the dance floor. The snake-head cane that belonged to Bill Kleitsch tapped against the floor as Bill and the sheriff made their way toward the front porch. Bill brushed against Rufus, but Rufus swiveled on his stool to keep fiddling.

After two more dances, it was time for a break. Rufus carefully balanced his fiddle and bow atop the stool, which he carried to a spot behind the bar for safekeeping. Most of the dancers wandered out to the porch to get ready for the fireworks though the tall stranger still stood in the middle of the dance floor, gazing adoringly at Maisie.

Rufus stopped to pick up and drink the one free beer the owner of The I allowed him.

The sun had set, and a large white disc of moon hung low in the darkening sky. Its light gleamed on the shiny black hood of Gilroy Tucker's Model B. Just the other side of the window behind the bar, Bill Kleitsch sat on the hickory bench with the sheriff, gabbing with two other men who'd straddled chairs in front of them. Bill grasped the brass head of his cane in one hand and his drink in the other.

"Here's tonight's pay," the bartender said, snapping Rufus away from the view outside and handing him two Liberty dimes. Rufus dropped these coins into the back pocket of his overalls, hearing them click against the metal gouge tool, then turned to make his way out to the porch.

"Where'd you get that?" the sheriff was asking Bill Kleitsch just as Rufus stepped through the open doorway.

"This?" Bill asked, holding up the whiskey-filled jar with a flourish.

Sheriff nodded, grinning. Knowing what was to come.

"Found it," Bill answered. "Mason lost it—his name's on it!"

The four men burst into loud laughter, even though they'd heard the joke many times before. Rufus knew better than to join in their laughter, but Bill scowled at him anyway.

"You ever see anything prettier than that?" Bill sneered.

"No siree," Rufus answered in his low voice, though he didn't know whether Bill meant the jar or his wife Maisie, who had remained inside with the tall stranger.

"You think she don't know who she's goin' home with tonight?"

Rufus lowered his eyes, not wanting trouble, not wanting to get caught in something that was none of his business. He stepped down into the yard and turned his attention to three men in white suits and straw hats kneeling at the closest corner of the parking lot, near a slab of rock. From where Rufus stood, they looked like they might be praying. But when one of the men shifted his position, Rufus saw three white dice shining in the moonlight on the rock before them.

Rufus watched the game a minute then turned back toward the porch. Maisie now stood backlit in the open doorway, the stranger towering behind her.

"I said, you think she don't know who she's goin' home with tonight?" Bill's voice carried across the yard. A pause then, louder. "I'm talking to you, fiddler."

"Hey now," the sheriff said. "No need to go on about it, Bill."

Rufus was used to being baited. He knew to ignore it. He'd come simply to play his fiddle. He'd been called every name in the book, but they rolled off his skin like drops of oil. Words didn't matter, Rufus figured. Only music did, and rhythm, and the touch of a woman, something he hadn't had since his wife died. Anything else wasn't worth getting upset about.

Rufus heard a noise up on The I's flat tin roof, where some boys sat with their new blue jeans dangling over the porch.

"I'm goin' inside to get another beer before the show starts," the sheriff said. "You keep yourself calm out here, Bill Kleitsch."

A whistling sound rose up behind Rufus.

Then, "Over there!" One of the boys, shouting from the roof.

There was a thunderous sound then, and Rufus turned to see a bright shower of fireworks light the sky beyond the parking lot and field. Flowers of gold, green, red burst into bloom. This was the first time Rufus had seen fireworks on the Fourth of July. He remembered as a boy seeing them used in the Negro part of town to celebrate Christmas. If they didn't have enough pennies to buy them, his uncle would blow air into a pig bladder, tie the organ tightly, and throw it on the fire for a satisfying explosion.

A trio of bangs then six streaks of light. Rufus stood with his head back, enjoying the show, until a hand clamped down on his shoulder and pulled him flat on his back on the ground.

He saw the bunched, gray fabric where Bill's left leg stopped just above knee-high and the snake-head cane. Rufus lifted a hand to protect himself, but it was too late. The cane battered his hand, his face, his chest. More explosions charged the air, and each time the fireworks burst bright, Bill's sneering face, filled with rage, was illuminated. Rufus twisted his body to roll away, but each time he moved, Bill pushed him back down. Bill straddled his chest, the stump of his leg scraping the gravel on one side of Rufus and the other intact leg bent back at an awkward angle. He'd dropped the cane, but now his fists pounded Rufus' head again and again until someone pulled him off and Rufus lay in the grass, trying to stay awake, alive, but finally giving up.

When Rufus woke, Augusta Sweet was kneeling beside him on the grass under a large oak tree. She clutched a blood-stained handkerchief in her hand. He felt bandages on his head and saw them on his hands. He tried to sit up and caught a glimpse of Bill Kleitsch maybe 20 yards away, back on the porch bench between the sheriff and Maisie, who was running two fingers down his cheek. Maisie's blond hair glowed as the sky burst into another field of bright flowers. The tall stranger leaned against the door, frowning in confusion as he stared at her and Bill. A salesman's bag rested at his feet.

Rufus was angry at all of them. Most of all Bill but also Maisie for playing with men's hearts the way she did and the sheriff for letting Bill get away with what he did and the tall stranger for coming to town and hoping to find love there. White folk could do whatever they wanted. White folk got away with things. And when some white person felt bad they took it out on the black man.

The crowd cheered. Rufus' stomach roiled, and his eyes burned, so he closed them again, hoping for darkness. Anger roared through him as he imagined the man killed last week by white farmworkers, the lynching of his own cousin in Hot Springs the year Rufus' wife died. He stirred on the grass, willing himself to rise and walk over to the porch, to lean into Bill and slip that gouge tool he always carried, the one he'd used to smooth and round the back of his fiddle, between Bill Kleitsch's ribs. The ribs would be white. He wanted to see them, rip them from the man's chest. He lay down again to get rid of the dizziness he felt, fully intending to rise and do the deed.

Someone touched him, and he flinched.

"Take this." It was Gilroy Tucker, easing his white linen jacket beneath Rufus' head.

Behind the publisher's shoulder, the bartender peered down.

"You okay?" he asked brusquely.

Rufus knew that fiddlers were a dime a dozen in Arkansas. Customers were not. But the fury inside him wouldn't go away. If he stabbed Bill, he'd lose his job. Might be lynched himself. But so be it. His wife gone, his parents gone, no children. All the days ahead were sure to be dark ones.

"I'm okay," he said, bracing himself against the ground and slowly rising to his feet. "I just want to step up there on the porch a minute. I got somethin' I gotta do."

Augusta Sweet suddenly rose to her full height beside him, stained handkerchief tight in her hand, frowning as she looked at him. Like she could she see what was inside him.

Gilroy Tucker said, "I'll drive you home, Rufus."

The sound of his name spoken so gently stunned Rufus. But he shook his head no and took a step toward the porch. He could feel the fiddle gouge pressing against his scrawny buttock.

Hands stopped him, and Augusta spun him around to face her. Those eyes, dark and wise. Holding him in place with one hand, she set the other on top of his left chest, where his heart beat. She closed her eyes, though Rufus saw them roll back in her head, behind the blue-veined lids. Her breaths slowed and deepened. Whether it was simply this second show of rare kindness from white folks or the magic touch of a bonesetter's hand, Rufus felt something sad and heavy begin to leave the prison of his aching chest.

Cheers arose from the crowd as more starbursts of color filled the sky like paper flowers blooming in a glass of water.

A shout came from the porch. The tall stranger stood above Bill, swinging a fist into his face, grabbing Maisie by the hand. The Mason jar fell to the ground, glass breaking.

"Bill," Maisie cried. And to the stranger, "No, I'm not a-goin' with you! What on earth you'd think that for? That's my husband you just punched."

The stranger stood still for a moment, eyes wide as the situation dawned on him. Then he turned and, picking up his travelling bag, stomped off the porch and out to the road, his tall form striding away from The I and all its temptations.

Rufus blinked. Augusta gave him a small smile.

"Let me drive you home," Gilroy Tucker said again, and Rufus nodded.

"Thank you, ma'am," he said to Augusta.

Augusta touched him above his heart once more, this time with a single finger. To his surprise, he placed his wrinkled black hand on top of hers.

"It helps to know there are others," she said.

He wasn't sure what she meant. Others who would come in and do the dirty work? Or others like her and Gilroy Tucker trying to make the world a better place, fight off evil?

Maybe she was saying his music was a way to do that, too.

"Thank you, ma'am," he said again, because he didn't know what else to say. Then he followed Gilroy Tucker out to the Model B. No one tried to stop them; everyone was too busy watching the sky. For a second he felt that old ire rise up then it slithered back down into the crevices of a dark cave inside him. Best to keep it there for now. He knew well enough that times like these, times of light and color, of music and dance, were what sustained folks, no matter what shade their skin. Tonight, fiddling, he'd been a part of that sustenance all folks need and wanted to keep it that way.

"You're a good man, Rufus," Gilroy Tucker said as he opened the front passenger door.

Rufus swallowed and climbed into the car then turned to the white-haired publisher. "You, too, Mr. Tucker."

The passenger door shut, and Rufus watched in the mirror as Gilroy Tucker walked around the back of the Ford. He climbed in behind the wheel, pulled back on the brake, and pushed a lever on the steering wheel.

"Key on. Gas on. Spark up."

The engine turned over, and Tucker pulled the lever between him and Rufus.

"I'll send a doctor over after I drop you off," he said. "You let me know if you need anything else, you hear?"

"Yes sir," Rufus answered and hummed softly along with the engine as the Model B carried him home.

"Morning Train" by Thomas Hart Benton

MORNING TRAIN

September 1942

When the draft notice came in the mail, the Order to Report for Induction signed by President Roosevelt himself, Ruthann Parker desperately hoped her son, Daniel, would be rejected. Maybe for his hearing, which had seemed to decline in recent years. But the test said his ears were fine, and Ruthann realized he simply tuned her and her husband, Virgil, out when he wanted to.

One July afternoon she tried to talk him out of going to war. She and Daniel were sitting on low stools in the victory garden they'd planted. Ruthann had wanted to speak to her son alone and knew that Virgil was probably drinking mountain dew, moonshine, at Corky Brown's that afternoon.

Daniel was on his knees, picking bright green peas from climbing vines. He rolled a pod between two fingers, pinched off both ends, and pulled the fine string on the inside. One by one he popped four peas into his mouth.

"Don't go," his mother said.

"Have to, Ma." Speaking to her in that new grown-up way he had.

"I don't want you to go."

"It's the right thing to do," he said. "I'd die for my country."

This was not what Ruthann wanted to have happen. She didn't understand how any mother could love her country more than her own son. But she didn't say anything.

She spent the rest of that summer canning what she could from the garden. When there was extra sugar at the store, she made pots of greengage and red currant jelly to keep for Christmas, like she always had. Ruthann convinced herself Daniel would still be home at the holidays, even as she watched cousin Gene, Benjamin Lee Bird, and Junior Orman leave for overseas.

Every morning Ruthann read the *St. Louis Post-Dispatch* and *Kansas City Journal-Post*, though Virgil said the newspapers were an unnecessary expense. She would buy the papers up at Gruber's grocery after she'd fed her two men and washed the dishes and made the beds and fed the cows, chickens, and pigs. Ruthann knew more about what was going on in the world than Virgil or Daniel did, and in fact, more than most of the folks in the small farm town did. This didn't make her proud; it made her lonely.

Ruthann had wanted to be a reporter once, like Helen Thomas. She'd even gone to college in St. Louis and later, when Daniel was 12, taken him there on a trip to see the zoo, with its bear pits and antelope house, walk-through birdcage, and the newly built Jewel Box, a huge fifty-foot high glass conservatory filled with hundreds of flowers, plants, and trees. She knew that before this new conservatory had been built, an early mayor had set up greenhouse displays to see which plants could survive despite the high levels of smoke and soot in the fast-growing city.

She and Daniel had taken a streetcar, green with yellow lettering on the side. Ruthann still remembers the number of the car: 33. There was a reflecting pool at the entrance to Forest Park and past that, the conservatory. You could walk around inside on a concrete balcony and see hundreds of flowers, plants, and trees, above and below you, all lit by sunshine streaming in through thousands of panes of glass set in verdigris wrought iron supports. There were hundreds of chrysanthemum laid out in a formal Chinese design. Trees that stretched toward an Art Deco roof. Baskets of flowering plants hanging from the ceiling. Roses growing up forest-green trellises, tall stalks of iris, even an orange tree growing like a miracle indoors.

It was a sight she would never forget, a cathedral of growing things.

The greenhouse had been much smaller when Ruthann first arrived in St. Louis. A classmate at university had taken her to see a special floral display there one Christmas. Later, she and this classmate kissed. Later still, he pushed Ruthann down on his gold leather sofa, and in nine months, her beautiful son was born, her college plans derailed, and her classmate nowhere to be seen. She remained in St. Louis, though, taking a job as a secretary at a farm equipment company and leaving Daniel in the care of a young woman with whom she shared a small apartment.

Virgil came in to the office one day, wearing his white Navy uniform, handsome and hopeful. He promised Ruthann she could go back to school one day. He promised that they would live on his family farm just a few years then return to the city. He promised that he loved both her and Daniel, and Ruthann accepted this as the significant gift it was.

The farm kept her busy, as did raising Daniel and tiptoeing around Virgil so as not to provoke his anger, which erupted frequently. Ruthann loved Virgil; she really did. But it wasn't long before she realized that she loved the man she hoped he *could* be rather than the man he was. Still, she was grateful for everything he'd given her and Daniel, grateful for the way he stepped in as Daniel's father. She didn't know exactly where Virgil's anger came from but wondered if something had happened to him during the War to leave him so wary and on edge. Whatever the cause of it, everything she tried to do to appease him failed.

And now, her only child was going to be taken away by Uncle Sam before she had anywhere near enough of him. Her own journey through life had been too fast, the consequence of her choices too unremitting. But if Uncle Sam was going to send her boy across the ocean to fight, she prayed to God that somehow he would escape whatever damage could come to him there.

In late August, Ruthann heard that cousin Gene had been among the first Marines to land on Guadalcanal. He wrote his mama about the bombers that flew over at noon, the dysentery and malaria, the banzai charges where hundreds of enemy troops attacked on foot.

"That boy did his family proud," Virgil said.

Ruthann shivered but stayed silent. At night, she began dreaming about the things Gene wrote in his letter: jungles and foxholes and a dead soldier he'd found floating in a river.

Then, before dawn one day in September, she and Virgil and Daniel found themselves on the train platform in Hannibal. She clutched Daniel's elbows, leaning into him and staring up at his face under the regulation square-topped cap he wore.

When he pulled away, Ruthann lost her balance. A snake writhed in her stomach. She didn't want Daniel to go to war. She didn't want his life to be colored by violence. Her stomach growled. She hadn't eaten though she'd put two big breakfasts out for her men: eggs from the henhouse, two cups of precious coffee, even beefsteak that took up the last of their red stamps though it was only mid-month. She had even brought a brown bag filled with the last of the bell peppers and carrots, hoping Daniel would take these parting gifts from the garden he had helped her plant.

Across the tracks, their dust-spattered gray Ford pickup waited for what would be a terribly sad trip home. Daniel had told her that the truck, with its vee grille, pointed hood, and fender-mounted headlights, would be the last of its kind. Because of the war, the government had ordered Ford to make only military Jeeps, aircraft engines, and bombers. Ruthann knew there were many other, better things the government could spend money on but as always, kept her thoughts to herself.

Behind the truck, a tall water tower rose. Daniel once told Ruthann how, during his high school years, he and Gene, Benjamin Lee, and Junior Ormon would climb the tower and sit high up there on the walkway at night, drinking Orange Crush and imagining their futures.

"These pants need pressing," Ruthann said, running her thumb gently down the slash front of Daniel's sage trousers.

"Too late for that, Mom." Daniel took a step back, signaling again that she simply couldn't keep him.

He was seventeen. And six-foot-two, so tall compared to her and Virgil. Tall like the classmate who'd made love to her on that gold couch.

The train tracks were hewn boards laid under iron rails that curved away as they left the station. The rails merged in the distance; behind them, a low hill rose, a slim crescent of sun at its top.

Virgil cleared his throat. That morning he'd sworn cusswords at Ruthann for knocking the sugar bowl off the table as she handed a duffel bag to Daniel. Sugar was rationed, and *they goddamn better take care of the little they had*, he had screamed. Ruthann cared about words; it was one reason she'd wanted to be a journalist. She hated hearing them used carelessly and cruelly.

The canvas duffel bag now stood on the platform, packed with undershirts and drawers that were the color of dirty green, as well as brown cotton socks, black sweaters. Pack straps, leggings, foot powder.

"You should reach St. Louis late afternoon, son," Virgil said.

Daniel scooted his cap back on his head, "New Wabash line runs up to eighty-five miles an hour."

Virgil let out a long, low whistle. One pocket of his short coat hung loose, and Ruthann reminded herself to mend it.

From St. Louis, Daniel would take a bus to the Jefferson Barracks in Lemay.

"You write me soon as you get your orders," Virgil said.

"Yes, sir." Daniel's coat was belted at the waist and reached just above his boots. His skin was still baby-faced, and dark hair curled above his ears. The Army would make him cut it, Ruthann knew.

"If I were you," Virgil said, "I'd sure as hell hope to go where the action is." He puffed up his chest like their Rhode Island Red rooster did each morning. "The Pacific. Solomon Islands. Fierce fighting going on there now. No use twiddling your thumbs at a desk."

Ruthann pulled a tomato from the bag, offered it to Daniel as though presenting it on a red velvet pillow.

"It's sweet enough you could eat it right now," she said.

Daniel kicked the duffel bag with one of his over-the-ankle boots. *Boondockers*—it had been a new word for her to learn. The language of men. "No, Ma," he said. "Not now."

When he saw the disappointment that must have rippled across her face, he added, "You took me to St. Louis once when I was little, right, Ma?"

She nodded and smiled, all slights forgiven.

"I don't remember much of what I saw, but I'm excited to see the city," he said. "Excited to see a lot of new places."

She nodded. She knew that feeling.

Virgil walked over to stare at a poster nailed to the station wall: *KEEP 'EM FLYING IS OUR BATTLE CRY! DO YOUR PART FOR DUTY - HONOR - COUNTRY.* A large circular Seth Thomas clock hung nearby: 5:16. Daniel's train would arrive soon. "Daniel, I wanted…" Ruthann's words trailed off, and neither her son nor husband questioned what she had been about to say.

"You pack my Cardinals cap, Ma?" Daniel asked. She nodded again. The cap was blue with a red bill.

"You'll watch the first game of the Series for me?" Daniel asked Virgil. "In case I'm somewhere I can't."

"You better believe it, son." Virgil smiled. A lovely smile, really. It was hard for Ruthann to reconcile his beautiful smiles with the curses he sometimes flung at her.

"Think Billy Southworth can keep our team on its winning streak?"

"Did a fine job against the Pirates last week."

"Yankees haven't lost a Series since '26," Daniel said.

Daniel was two that year—with long curls Ruthann had refused to cut, sweet giggles as he stood in his crib in ABC pajamas in the mornings.

Above the train tracks, pink ribbons had painted the sky. A full circle of sun now posed on the horizon, a small dark smudge at its center.

"Kuroski and that new kid Beazley will save us. We had too many injuries last year. But you'll see," Virgil said.

"Hope you're right," Daniel said and then looked at Ruthann. "There'll be plenty to keep you busy, too, Ma. You won't even notice I'm gone."

She knew this wouldn't be true. Knew there would be a huge hole once Daniel left. One she wasn't sure Virgil could fill.

Her husband pushed his hat up. "Boy's reminding me we're out of beer, Ruthann." Beer was another thing that drew out Virgil's rage. Alcohol content was down because of grain rationing, so when Virgil drank, he had to drink many bottles, and his supply went down quickly.

When Ruthann didn't answer, Daniel cleared his throat. "What happened to the window in the garden shed?" he asked. "Saw it this morning as we got in the truck. Looks like somebody took a sledgehammer to it."

Not a hammer, Ruthann thought. A pumpkin. Last night, while Daniel was asleep on the other side of the house, Virgil, in a drunken rage, had thrown one at the little shed he'd built for her garden.

"You'll get the window fixed before cold weather sets in, right, Pa?"

Virgil had gone drinking at Corky's, and it was long past midnight when Ruthann heard him pull up in the truck. She'd stood with her hands against their second story bedroom window as she watched her husband stagger into the garden. He looked like a madman, his hat pulled low, his work boots dancing crazily, stepping in this row of squash and that row of cabbage. Getting his foot caught in pumpkin vines and ripping them out of the dirt. He bent and when he stood up, he held a still-green pumpkin in his hand. He turned, stumbling, and then lifted his arm and moved it around and around in circles like a pitcher loosening up on the mound. As the pumpkin flew from his hand, Ruthann couldn't hear a thing, but she saw pieces of glass fall near the shed, each one holding a sliver of fractured moonlight.

Virgil grunted and pulled a bent cigarette from his pocket and then turned away to light it.

"I wonder if you'll have any time to spare in St. Louis," Ruthann said to Daniel. "You could go see the Jewel Box."

Virgil snorted, and even Daniel looked embarrassed.

"No time for that," Virgil said as his smile turned into a sneer. "He's a man, not a boy. He's going to save our country."

But there were many things worth saving, Ruthann thought, as the snake looped again through her insides.

The minute hand on clock had moved The dark smudge inside the sun had turned into something recognizable, a train traveling swiftly toward them. Smoke billowed from its stack, and its melancholy whistle shouted its code: short, short, long, short.

She threw her arms around her son's neck and hugged him tight, not wanting to let him go.

"Ma," he whispered down into her hair.

Then the train arrived—a massive black beast of metal and smoke, with its deafening high-pitched shriek. Come to take her son, her hope, away.

The doors opened on a conductor in blue shirt and pants. "All aboard," he said not knowing or caring how those words could change lives forever.

"Pa," Daniel said to Virgil. "Take care of Ma."

A cry escaped Ruthann, but it was hidden in the howl of the train.

"Go on now, get on board," Virgil shouted, and Daniel climbed up one, two, three steps into the maw between two cars.

He turned to face them, duffel bag in hand.

"You forgot the food!" Ruthann shouted, holding out the paper bag of vegetables. She planted and cared for them so carefully, carried them here to the station.

Daniel shook his head.

Virgil lit a cigarette, blowing its smoke up into the sky.

Once more the conductor shouted, "All aboard!" Then he pulled up the stairs. Daniel shifted out of view, then returned. He winked as the wheels turned slowly and began to pick up speed. Ruthann kept her eyes glued to Daniel's body leaning out of the vanishing train until she couldn't see him anymore. As the train cars passed by, she felt waves of hot air press against her body, almost knocking her over.

"Go get 'em, killer!" Virgil shouted.

"I feel sick," Ruthann said and ran inside the station, past one of the new Coca-Cola coolers and past a metal rack of train schedules. In the Ladies Room, she wanted to vomit but couldn't, just spat into the sink a few times, all the while gulping down sobs. Then she splashed cold water on her face and walked back out, stopping at the rack to take one of the train schedules. It was cream-colored, with a red starburst. Missouri Pacific Lines. A line drawing of a train with a curved line behind it showing a mountain and the words "Over there."

She stuffed it into the pocket of her coat then walked out to where she found Virgil sitting in their truck, arms atop the steering wheel, head down.

Neither of them spoke. She rolled the window down for fresh air. Halfway through the drive home, they found themselves behind a truck that was going too slow. Virgil blasted the horn once, twice, three times, and swore a blue streak. Ruthann stared at his profile, at his tightly furrowed brow, jutting chin. She had been so eager to love him. So hopeful. But every obscenity he said, every angry curse he shouted, had pushed her farther away until there was nothing but a wide gap between them. Like the space between the train cars Daniel had just filled.

When Virgil turned to look at her, she finally saw something in his eyes that made her realize there was only one place that much anger could have come from, and that was sorrow.

She said, "Let's stop and get you some beers, Virgil."

If he drank, he would fall asleep early. She could go out to the garden to repair the damage he'd done, then make him dinner, mend that ripped pocket on his coat.

Thinking of the pocket reminded her of the train schedule. Missouri Pacific Lines, the railroad that could take her to St. Louis. She thought of the Jewel Box, of all the glorious plants that had grown there, protected from the soot of the city. The exotic birds that flew above them. It was a sight she'd never forget, a cathedral of living things. The animals she'd seen in the park, brought from far across the ocean her son would soon cross. A sacred cow, called a zebu, and a Moorish bridge.

A child had been born, another marvel.

A child Virgil had helped her raise, even if imperfectly.

Maybe one day soon she would visit the Jewel Box again. Maybe she would ask Virgil to join her, to take a trip away from everything they'd known to date. She didn't know if he would want to go, or if he would appreciate the wonders of the Jewel Box, and even worse, what she would do if he didn't.

"It took my breath away," she said softly to the air outside the truck window. "You'll see."

"The Meeting" by Thomas Hart Benton

Pointing East, Where Things Happen

Arkansas, 1922

Helen was surprised when her Aunt Abitha suggested she attend the evening service over in Beaver Creek.

"Beaver Creek's a good half hour's ride, Aunty. And Walter hates going to church," Helen said, continuing to swipe Fels-Naptha in angry strokes on a windowsill in her kitchen

"It would do your husband good," Abitha said. She stood near the counter staring at the carton that had originally held 10 bars of the soap. Only two remained since the women had been cleaning all week. "Do you all some good, I'd wager."

"Give me that," Helen said, more abruptly than she'd intended.

Abitha raised an eyebrow, holding the red-and-black carton to her chest. "This? Where'd you find it anyway? Never seen a big box like this."

"Walter picked it up at the Woolworth's last weekend," Helen said. "Among other things." She scowled and grabbed the carton from her aunt's pudgy fingers then slipped the last bar out. After unwrapping it, she grated shavings into a glass bowl with an inch of water in its base.

"Works wonders, doesn't it?" Abitha said. "On stains and more." She popped a fresh-baked shortbread cookie into her mouth then wiped her hands on the gingham apron stretched across her large stomach. "When your mother and I were wee young things, *our* Mama used to make it into a paste and spread it on our poison ivy."

At the mention of her mother, Helen wanted to cry. It had been just a month since she'd died unexpectedly of a heart attack. Helen wanted to talk to her, tell her about Bucky's and Walter's latest shenanigans.

With a spoon, Helen swirled the bright orange and yellow flakes in circles in the water. Abitha started reading off the carton: "The Golden Bar with the Clean Naptha Odor. Your house will be cleaner; your work easier; and your health, and that of your family, safeguarded."

"Pshaw." Helen dipped a towel in the soapy water and went to attack another window frame. She was tired. Nothing could clean up the sadness she lived in, she thought. "Bucky'll be here soon. I've got to get dinner on."

Soon as the words left her mouth, she wished she hadn't said them. Sure enough, her aunt took it as an invitation.

"I'll whip up fried chicken and scalloped potatoes for us," Abitha said.

"No, no. That's not necessary. And besides, it's too hot to eat that much." Helen peered through the window at the buckboard wagon waiting there. "Anyway, Walter will be driving you home soon. I can manage." She was thinking she could give Bucky some of that potato soup she'd made. Cut up a slice of cold ham to drop in.

She turned, saw the disappointment on her aunt's face. "We'll have a real Sunday dinner next time." She walked to undo the ties of the gingham apron and pat her aunt's powdered and rouged cheek. "Now tell me about this travelling preacher again."

Abitha brightened. "He'll only be here a short while. I saw a flyer in town at the post office: '2 Weeks of Preaching, Testimony, Bible Study & Fellowship,' it said. 'Preacher Zebediah Corne Presiding.' He'll be in Beaver Creek tomorrow night.

"Why's he so special?"

"Your mama and I heard him preach at camp meetings when we was girls," the older woman said. "Happiest I've ever seen folks in church."

A horse neighed outside. Walter was walking toward the wagon, leading their mare Lady Ghost behind him. Walter was tall, broad-shouldered, his hair gray at the temples. A handsome man, Helen thought. One any woman would want.

The front screen door slammed, and Bucky burst into the kitchen, dropping his books in their leather strap on the wooden counter and grabbing half a dozen cookies.

"There's my boy!" Abitha grabbed the 12-year-old to her bosom; the cookies dropped to the brown-and-gray patterned linoleum.

When Bucky squirmed away, Helen saw several fingers on his left hand were taped onto popsicle stick splints.

Helen blinked, momentarily torn between the mess on the floor and the splints.

Abitha jumped in. "I'll get the dustpan," she said and headed toward the pantry.

"Got my fingers caught in the art cabinet," Bucky mumbled, looking down at the floor. "Orice slammed it on me."

Helen sighed, certain there was more to the story. Bucky had gone wild this year, getting into trouble every other week and talking back to both her and his teachers. Pulling the braids on their widowed neighbor's pretty daughter, Orice. Once even getting caught kissing her on the playground.

"How is that nice neighbor of yours doing, Helen?" Abitha asked. "Orice's father. He seemed so sad last time I saw him."

Their neighbors had moved into the small shack a mile down the dirt road only a year before, after Randall's wife had died of typhus, leaving him with their little girl. Walter told Helen how thousands of soldiers had died during the war, how the infection had been spread by lice on rats and raccoons, even cats. It was important to stay clean, he said.

Helen glanced outside. Walter had reached the wagon now and was hitching up Ghost Lady.

"His wife did die, Aunty. He's got good cause to be sad. And his girl's gone a bit wild, too, if you ask me, though that's no excuse to torment her." She scowled at Bucky then turned back to her aunt who still stood in the doorway of the pantry. "Go on now, Aunt Abitha, Walter's out there waiting for you. We'll handle this," Helen said and grabbed the dustpan and shoved it into Bucky's good hand.

"But you'll come to evening service tomorrow night? Promise me?" Abitha asked.

"Yes, yes, I'm sorry." Helen felt she would burst into tears if she had to say more. "Yes, we'll pick you up tomorrow at 4 then go to church." *For Mama's sake,* Helen thought. *And mine.*

Even a month after her mother's death, Helen was still moping around too much, Walter told her. Which is why he'd asked Aunt Abitha to come help her clean the house. He didn't know what else to do with her, he said.

Helen and her mother had often talked about Walter, how sometimes he seemed so unable to see what people needed in their hearts. It was like there were two levels to living, Helen thought. The one where the fields got plowed and animals were bred. And the one below that people didn't talk much about, where folks often needed a tenderness Walter wasn't always skilled at showing.

Still, there were those chores that needed doing. The horses had to be fed; milk, eggs, and chicken taken into town to sell; and the cows checked for pregnancy and culled. That summer's meager crop of fruits had to be canned, mincemeat and sausage pudding made.

When they met, Walter had wooed Helen something mighty. It had been glorious those early years. And, because she loved him, Helen had pushed aside her mother's disapproval that Walter was sometimes a little too rough-edged.

"I heard you yelp when he grabbed your arm last night," she'd said once after they'd all gone to dinner in town. "Man shouldn't treat a woman like that."

"It's nothing, Mama," Helen had answered, not knowing why she always defended Walter except that he could be gentle when he wanted to be and loved her more than she'd ever been loved. She'd wanted desperately for him to be the man she imagined him to be.

But things changed for the worse when Bucky was born. Walter was around less, more focused on his job at the sawmill factory. Always tired and cranky when he got home. More stressed as his responsibilities grew. Wanting to make love even when Helen was tired. Wanting her attention to be focused on him, not Bucky.

Helen knew that as much as Walter loved their son, he slightly resented the fact that someone else now had a place in her heart, which heretofore had been reserved exclusively for him. A few years ago, Helen saw him behind the post office, kissing a woman she didn't know. Walter had opened her heart wide and with that kiss, broken it. When she confronted him, Walter told her over and over that he loved her more than the other woman and that if she only loved him the way he wanted her to, he would never stray again.

Helen knew something was wrong with those words, but she kept trying. She trusted he would be faithful, and things would be different.

And they had been, for the most part.

He continued to flirt with women in town, though.

"I swear," she'd told her mother one afternoon when Bucky was a handful. "I don't fathom how a smart man can be so clumsy in the realm of the heart. I saw Walter flirting up a storm with that new clerk at the Five & Dime. When I told him I'd seen him, he acted like a little boy—" She'd gestured toward Bucky running as fast as his chubby legs would carry him. "Like a little boy who's been caught with his hand in the cookie jar, innocent and guilty and proud all at the same time."

Helen would occasionally grow tired of her suspicions about her husband's fidelity, tired of her son's rudeness, and she'd put some dresses and underthings and shoes in her suitcase, tying the gold ribbons to keep everything in place.

But for nearly a year now, Walter had been coming home early in the evenings. They'd listen to the new radio station WOK, the news bulletins and ads offering appliances guaranteed to "lift burdens." There were weekly sermons from a Dr. Trimble of Lakeside Methodist Church and musical shows broadcast from Pine Bluffs. Sometimes, after Bucky had gone to bed, Walter took Helen in his arms, and they danced till midnight in the parlor.

But since her mother's death, Helen hadn't felt like dancing.

"We can listen to Dr. Trimble on the radio a hell of a lot easier," Walter had said when Helen first told him about Abitha's invitation. But then he'd invited their neighbor Randall and his daughter Orice to go with them.

"Are you sure that's a good idea?" Helen asked. "Bucky will be bound to act up then, and I can't face him making a disturbance at church. I really can't."

"He'll be fine," Walter said. "I'll keep an eye on the young Buck. And Randall's been looking morose lately. Anniversary of his wife's death's coming up next week, you know."

Helen found the tiny box just before they left for Beaver Creek. She'd decided to wear her seersucker dress, white on top and blue-and-white striped in the skirt, and had stood on a stepstool to reach the top shelf of the closet she and Walter shared. There was a straw hat with white ribbon there, sitting atop her tweed suitcase. The box, dark blue with a pink ribbon, fell to her feet when she moved the suitcase reaching for her hat.

Inside the box, a gold filigree bracelet lay on puffed white satin. A pretty bracelet that was far too small for her own wrist.

Helen quickly calculated. There was no birthday coming up, and it was months until Christmas. Besides, Walter had a history that didn't promote trust.

This time, she thought, his stupid, charming ways might have gone beyond mere shenanigans.

She'd confront him soon as they got home from Beaver Creek, she decided. In the meantime, she pulled the suitcase down to start planning her escape.

Walter yelled up the stairs. "Lady Ghost and I are waiting."

Helen arranged the straw hat carefully on her hair, freshened her lipstick, and walked down, silent and stunned. She saw Walter wink at her from where he sat on the buckboard but didn't respond as she joined Bucky, who was barefoot and in overalls, in the back of the wagon. When they reached the neighbors', Randall and Orice stood in front of their small shack, two scrawny beanpoles who looked like they didn't know where on earth they now belonged. Helen thought at once that she should have come over earlier and offered to iron poor Orice's dress, with its red scalloped trim on the neck and puffed sleeves. There were things Randall couldn't be expected to know to do.

Randall and Orice sat themselves on the bench across from Helen and Bucky, and Helen held Bucky's non-bandaged hand on her lap during the half hour ride. Still, he managed to send at least one spitball Orice's way. Randall didn't notice and stayed quiet during the long ride, even after they picked up Aunt Abitha who talked nonstop, unaware of her niece's agony. Like her father, Orice spent most of the time looking down at the floor, only occasionally glancing up at Bucky and grinning.

A log cabin stood in the middle of the campground, surrounded by a half dozen tents. Nearby was a brush arbor, a wooden framework covered with vines, and a large tire swing hanging from a tall oak. They made their way into the cabin, where Aunt Abitha moved quickly to sit on a stool at the side of the room near a window. She pointed to the wooden benches up front, saying "You all sit there. I need the breeze. Preacher'll be out in a second."

The birch pews were covered with leaflets. Helen picked one up and to distract herself from thoughts of the bracelet, read the towns the itinerant preacher would visit that month: Warnock Springs, Midway, Gravelly, Mt. Pleasant, Bethel, Red Colony, Keener. There was a schedule for that day as well, noting that after the evening's worship service cool drinks and ice cream would be served.

A dozen other folks had come to hear the preacher. Helen recognized the Marston brothers sitting behind the makeshift pulpit. The two men had built the pine coffin for her mother. Tears threatened to spill, but Bucky wriggled at her side, and before she knew it he was off the bench, running around the cabin.

"Don't worry," Aunt Abitha called over. "Let him be. Boy's got to get that out of his system before the preacher comes in."

With Bucky no longer between them, Helen could feel the warmth and weight of Walter's body next to hers. She could feel the muscles in his thighs through her dress and felt both longing and anger.

Bucky scrambled up into the empty space next to Orice. Helen hissed, "Bucky, get back here."

To her surprise, Randall reached up from the bench behind her and briefly rested his hand on her shoulder. "He's not bothering anybody."

Walter snorted loudly and turned around to face Randall. "Not now anyways. Christ, that boy's a handful. Showing off for your girl, I 'magine." He grabbed the boy by one arm, pulling him onto his lap. Helen pursed her lips and refused to look at either of them.

She'd always turned to her mother when bad things happened. Somehow that made life better, because she'd come to realize that it was the secrets that locked up her insides and made her pretend to sleep, pulling away from a man she wanted so much to trust. But now, her Mama was gone.

Preacher Zebediah Corne suddenly strode to the front of the room. It could be none other. He was the skinniest man Helen had ever seen, with bones protruding everywhere—his jaw, his elbows, those unnaturally long fingers.

The preacher reached behind Aunt Abitha to push the tall window further open; a breeze ruffled the woman's gray silk bonnet. Behind her, Helen could just make out the Arkansas hills in the fading light.

"Fresh air is as good for the soul as the body!" Preacher Corne shouted, and a few voices murmured their agreement.

"But never ignore the darkening sky!" the preacher thundered as he strode back to the pulpit. "In the darkness who among us can see? Who seeth us?" Each word he shouted stretched out with such intensity that Helen half-expected the letters themselves to hang in the air before the odd man's open mouth.

She closed her eyes, not wanting to listen. All she could think about was the bracelet. She tried to think which of several women Walter might be wooing. There was the new postmistress, a pretty young thing with auburn hair who'd just moved to town from the next county. Or one of the salesgirls at Woolworth's, standing behind a glass-topped counter, wearing bright lipstick and a ready smile. Or even Jenny Brackman who ran the combination General Store & Tavern.

She'd wanted so much for Walter to love her like she'd first imagined he did. Love her despite her sorrows and worries. She wanted his flirtations to stop, the charm he directed at most women he spoke to, even when Helen stood nearby. There'd been nothing specific Helen could rationally object to, and he always made light of her concerns, but she'd seen what she'd seen. Felt what she'd felt. A woman senses these things. And Walter had that radiant smile, those eyes bright as heaven when they shone on you.

But if Walter had grown impatient and once again looked for love elsewhere, this surely had to be the last straw. At least she owed her mother that.

There was a snore from one of the Marston brothers; it was hard to tell which one though Brady Marston's head was bobbing.

Helen had lost track of what the preacher was saying. He stood up there, pointing toward the eastern wall where there was no window, only uneven split logs. The brothers Marston, both overweight and doughy, slumped against the wall, in their well-worn denim overalls and long-sleeved white shirts, fast asleep. In contrast, Helen's mind skittered about like the black-tailed jackrabbit that had run through the yard that morning, its long ears alert for predators, zigzagging here and there as though it had no idea where to go for real safety.

Helen forced her attention back to the preacher. He had stepped out from behind the pulpit and was holding a big black leather Bible, edged in gilt.

"Here is a call for the endurance of the saints, those who keep the commandments of God and their faith in Jesus," he said, emphasizing some words with a thump of his hand on the book.

Walter cleared his throat and shifted his legs. Bucky squirmed to get comfortable again on his father's lap, and Walter reached into his pocket, pulled something out, and slipped it into Bucky's hand, silencing him with a finger to his lips.

From behind them, Orice giggled. Randall said "Sshhh, sweetheart, sshhh" in that quiet, sad way of his. Helen pictured Randall putting his arm around his daughter and on Orice's other side, that dreadful empty place on the bench where Randall's poor dead wife would have sat.

Bucky squirmed again on Walter's lap. Walter grabbed the boy's tiny wrist, squeezed it hard enough for Bucky to say "Ouch."

The preacher glanced down then quickly moved his eyes back up and to the side, toward that far horizon where whatever he was promising lay.

"I'm bored," Bucky said in a loud whisper.

Helen sighed. Walter glanced at her, brows furrowed. She closed her eyes and shook her head to say *Nothing, everything's fine* because she had to pretend that it was, at least for now. She wouldn't confront him here in this makeshift church. Not with the preacher preaching and all these people around them come for nourishment for the soul, not sordid revelations about bracelets.

"This is what the Lord sayest," the preacher's voice suddenly boomed, with his eyes closed, his mouth open, and those uncanny fingers, still pointing somewhere Helen couldn't see. "Sometimes you have to go through the wilderness before you get to the Promised Land," the preacher thundered.

Behind Aunt Abitha, the sun was lower now, the sky gray, with a pale pink ribbon of light. Such an odd, true thing, Helen thought. That there could be such a delicate line of beauty woven in among the somber twilight.

"I want Jesus to become King of your heart," the preacher was saying. "Not just in theory. In practice."

Helen wasn't sure what she believed. She knew she wasn't perfect, nor were her husband and son, but she couldn't imagine that they would all go to hell just because Walter sometimes flirted or she sometimes pulled away from his touch. Even the church seemed another place she had to keep such secrets locked inside her.

Helen saw the pinch mark on Bucky's wrist where Walter had squeezed it, then watched as Walter laid his lips on her son's forehead. At first, Helen had had trouble understanding her husband could be both good and bad. Now she wondered if anyone could ever be otherwise.

She hadn't wanted to stay at the picnic after the service but Bucky whined so, and Randall pouted, almost as sourly as his daughter, so Helen agreed.

Bucky and Orice immediately ran to a large truck tire swing hung from the branch of an old oak. The grown-ups stood to the side, awkward. Abitha joined two other women beside a tall blue Eskimo Pie thermos cooler.

"Saw there's a sale at Woolworth's," Walter said to no one in particular. "OB sleeves and gloves to check the cows. Figure I'll head in first thing tomorrow morning."

Helen swallowed. The new clerk, pretty, fresh-faced.

Randall remained silent, and Helen thought how much it must

hurt to not have his wife by his side at night.

Helen heard the children laughing and turned to see Bucky push Orice too high in the swing, running under it so the girl squealed, her matchstick legs sticking out from under that wrinkled dress. Dirt coated the soles of the girl's feet.

"Bucky Blyeth, don't you kill me up here!" the girl sing-sang in her sweet voice, teasingly. "Don't you kill me, Bucky Blyeth!" She was grinning widely. "I'll sic my Pa on you if you do."

She stood waiting for Walter to say something, anything.

But he didn't.

Instead, he climbed down and walked to the swing. Randall sat, dejected, on a log, head in hands.

Walter caught the chain of the swing, slowed it to a safer speed. Then he winked at Bucky and pointed to his son's pocket.

Bucky pulled out the dark blue box tied with a pink ribbon. Helen watched, lips parted, as her son handed the box to Orice in her wrinkled, dirty dress. Watched as the box was opened and the girl's mouth shaped itself into an O. Orice gazed at Bucky with wide eyes then leaned forward to kiss him, very quickly and lightly, on the lips.

Walter turned and smiled at Helen. A white moon big as a dinner plate hung over the tall oak, washing its black-green leaves and the tire and its thick twisted rope in light.

Later, when Walter giddy-upped Ghost Lady, and they were all in the wagon heading home, Helen listened as the sounds of children playing and folks singing faded into the distance behind them as they left the campgrounds. This was the way her mother's memory would fade, too, she knew. All that sweetness grow distant behind her. Helen figured that Bucky would remember her Mama, but only a little, a wavering presence.

When they pulled up to Randall and Orice's shack, after dropping Aunt Abitha back at her home, Helen told Randall to bring the girl's dress over the next morning so she could remove the ice cream stain on its front. "I've got something that might take care of that," she said, remembering the box of Fels-Naptha and all it had promised to banish: chocolate, lipstick, tattle-tale gray. "All is forgiven!" the ads had proclaimed.

"Goin' Home" by Thomas Hart Benton

FOR HER OWN GOOD

Sedalia, Missouri 1939

Of all Bonnie's chores at the farm, gathering eggs was the one she most hated. She didn't like chickens, and the smell inside the coop turned her stomach. When a hen was setting on her nest, if Bonnie came too close, the bird would shriek and her feathers puff. Pa said the hens had a calling to brood, and it was natural for them to want to protect their eggs.

That morning, Bonnie, who was twelve, searched first for the eggs that had no chicken laying on them and found three to set gently in the basket she carried over one arm. As she did so, she heard a scream, not from one of the hens, but from a woman—it sounded like her mother—outside.

Stepping over the threshold built to keep the baby chicks inside, she saw Pa and Doc Alport leading her Mama down the stone path that led from their farmhouse to the dirt road. The path was lined with pretty pink flowers she and Mama had planted that spring. Out on the road, a big black car waited, its engine idling. Bonnie dropped the basket with its three eggs and ran.

"Mama, where are you going?" she cried out, but by the time she reached the road, the car had pulled away, dust tails flying behind it. Mama's hands pressed against the rear window, frantic, her mouth saying words Bonnie couldn't hear. Bonnie stood in the middle of the road, waving her arms and yelling until the car was out of sight.

Then she ran inside the house where Pa had disappeared. He sat at the kitchen table, drinking a beer, even though they hadn't had breakfast yet. Her little brother Cyrus had climbed on a tall stool by the sink and was staring out the window toward the road. Tears streaked his cheeks.

"Where's Mama going?" Bonnie asked, trembling. "What's wrong?"

Pa shook his head and took another gulp from the brown glass bottle. Its label, red and yellow, read Chubby Lager.

"Where's Mama?" Bonnie asked again. Her voice was high and wild. "Where's my Mama gone?" She stood next to him, her hands gripping the table to control their shaking. Pa reached up and slapped her cheek. Her eyes widened, and Cyrus jumped down from the stool to come to her side. "Pa," he whispered. "Bonnie didn't do nothin'." And then, "We'll go get the eggs, right, Bonnie? You left the basket out there?"

Cyrus tried to pull Bonnie away from the table, but before she had moved, Pa stood. Her cheek burned, and her breaths came fast.

"Your Ma has women's problems," Pa said. "Problems I ain't got time for."

And that was that.

Two days later, Aunt Rose, Mama's sister, came to visit all the way from Prairie. She reassured Bonnie and Cyrus their mother would be back home soon. She'd needed a little rest, Rose said. Bonnie saw tears brim in her aunt's eyes but was relieved they didn't fall. While Bonnie loved her Aunt, and had enjoyed happy times with her when her Mama was around, this was different. Bonnie didn't want a replacement for her mother, so she kept a careful distance from her aunt. Rose barely spoke a word to Pa, usually leaving a room when he entered, turning the radio up loud when he spoke. She would listen to the radio several hours a day. She liked *When a Girl Marries* and the new show *The Adventures of Ellery Queen*. Mama always listened to KRDO, and Bonnie was grateful Aunt Rose never moved the dial.

The details of that morning—the shape of her mother's mouth in a silent scream, the splay of her mother's fingers against the rear window of that black car—went in and out of focus in Bonnie's mind, as though she were turning the knob on one of the microscopes they used in science class. A simple turn could make whatever was on the glass rectangle—a yellow feather from a warbler, a hair from one of the girls in her class, a drop of blood—look clear and up close then blurred and far away. Most of the time Bonnie tried to keep the images of her Mama blurred and far away though she had nightmares of women screaming. She started biting her nails.

Somehow Bonnie managed to finish the last weeks of school.

"Your Mama would be proud," Aunt Rose said when Bonnie brought her report card home, three weeks after Mama had been taken away. Bonnie was especially glad she had beat out Marlene Pierce, Rose Singleton, and Edith McCullar for top honors in high sixth grade.

Marlene, Rose, and Edith were what Pa called fancy girls. They all wore store-bought dresses, knee stockings, and oxford or high-top shoes. Bonnie wore handsewn clothes and had to make do with one pair of shoes until they fell apart. Mama used to slip cardboard inside to cover holes in the soles.

Aunt Rose cooked meals for them during her visit—creamed chip beef on toast, baked apples, noodles with stewed tomatoes and corn Mama had canned last fall, fried potatoes with chopped onions and sliced hot dogs added at the last minute. This last was a favorite of Cyrus'. One morning, Rose asked Bonnie into her room and motioned for her to sit down at the dressing table. She hesitated but had nothing better to do that boring summer day so did as she was told. She sat in front of a rosewood-framed mirror, dismayed by her pale skin and wayward hair.

"Let's brighten you up a bit." Rose held out a cream-colored box with five small tubes of lipstick: Noir Red, Cherry Red, Red Velvet, Chocolate Kiss, and Dusty Rose. After studying Bonnie's reflection in the mirror, and running five streaks of color on the inside of her niece's wrist, Rose selected one of the metallic gold tubes, re-opened it, and held it under Bonnie's eyes. "Besame Cosmetics. The only brand we carry at Madame Martine's."

Bonnie had been to the beauty parlor where her aunt worked on more than one occasion, but she'd never been allowed to try on lipstick.

"This one's Dusty Rose," her aunt said. "Also perfect because it will help you remember me." Bonnie started to turn around in her seat, but her aunt stopped her.

"Pucker up."

Bonnie made a fish mouth in the mirror and watched the reflection of Aunt Rose as the woman who looked so like her Mama—auburn hair, tender eyes—used the angled tip to first line her lips then fill them in with the flat edge of the lipstick. Next she used a brush to get mascara from a red tin box and carefully applied this to Bonnie's top lashes.

Bonnie blinked.

"Like it?" Aunt Rose said. "You look lovely." Then she combed Bonnie's hair into a side parting wave and secured it with bobby pins.

"Now ain't that pretty?" she asked, and Bonnie smiled at her reflection in the mirror. Jimmy Steadman, who had given her a pink glass pendant earlier that summer, was sure to like her even more now. She hadn't seen him in the weeks since Mama left, and she didn't know why.

"Speaking of Madame Martine's," Aunt Rose said, hesitating. "I have to go back there today, honey. I'm sorry but they need me, too."

Bonnie stopped smiling, glanced up at her aunt reflected in the mirror. "Don't go," she said.

"You'll come visit me in Prairie real soon," Rose said later as they stood on the front porch with her marble blue metal suitcase all packed. "I'll give you a real special hairdo with the permanent wave machine."

"The one that's like a giant spider from outer space?" Cyrus asked.

"That's the one," Aunt Rose said, bending down to hug him.

Then she shooed Bonnie and Cyrus back inside the house and stepped into the yard where Pa stood waiting, arms akimbo, to take her to the train station in town. Bonnie couldn't hear what they said, but Aunt Rose's face was stern, and it wasn't long before Pa's arms had dropped. Rose's finger pointed under Pa's nose and thump, thump, thumped the air. Finally she motioned for him to get the suitcase and put it in the cart. She looked back at Bonnie and Cyrus peering through the kitchen window and said some more things to Pa. He shrugged.

Rose walked back to the porch, and Bonnie and Cyrus rushed out to wrap their arms around her. "Your Pa says you can come with us. And since I heard the Pettis County Fair has come to town, and the fairgrounds are by the station, he said you can go."

"We can?" Cyrus cried out. "We can?"

Bonnie couldn't believe it. "Aunt Rose, thank you!" she said. Then, remembering her dusty, worn jumpsuit, she asked, "Do you think I could change my clothes? Please?" Rose nodded, turning to wag her finger again at Pa, warning him not to complain.

Bonnie ran into her room to find the dress she already had in mind. The bright pink and blue feedsack dress with ruffle sleeves Mama had sewn for her to wear to church last Easter. It had a v-neck which would be perfect for showing off the pink glass pendant Jimmy had given her. He was bound to be at the Fair, and she wanted to look her best. She pulled the dress over her head, being careful not to muss her hair or move the bobby pins.

"Just sit still Cyrus," Bonnie said when he started kicking his bare feet in rhythm on the bumpy ride into town. They sat in the back bed of the donkey cart with Rose's suitcase, while the adults sat up front facing forward. She didn't like that she could see only things they had already passed: rows of knee-high corn. A corrugated metal silo. Half a dozen Red Angus heifers and a stout bull.

"We learned in Sunday School…" Bonnie started.

"You mean when Mama took us? When's Mama coming home, Bonnie?" Cyrus asked.

"I don't know." She stared at the red cows. "In the Bible red heifers were killed as a sacrifice. It had to be a perfect cow, without anything wrong with it."

"What's a heifer?" Cyrus asked.

"A cow, silly. Like those over there." She cleared her throat. "A heifer is a cow that hasn't had a calf yet."

Cyrus started to whistle, a new skill he showed off every chance he got. Bonnie nudged him.

"Stop it," she whispered, nodding toward Pa. "He'll hear you. You know he don't like you doing that."

So Cyrus stopped, and the two of them listened to the slow creak of the cart's wheels.

Cyrus, in overalls and a blue-checked shirt, propped his cheek on his hand. "He won't get mad. Not today. Not with the Fair."

Long, gray clouds streaked the sky, but Bonnie still hoped it wouldn't rain. She didn't want anything to ruin the day.

When the cart reached town, Pa pulled up to a post in front of Dee's Market, a block down from the train station. This was where Mama used to buy their groceries. That day the front window held painted signs for baked beans, two for a quarter, and rows of Rice Krispies boxes and Lux Laundry Soap. Mama used to let Bonnie and Cyrus buy a penny orange when they behaved well as she shopped.

Pa took down the suitcase and set it at Rose's feet. Bonnie and

Cyrus started to jump down to give Aunt Rose one more hug, but Pa said no, they were to stay put. Rose put her fingers to her lips and blew kisses then pursing her lips, turned and walked away toward the train station.

Bonnie wanted to cry so bad. And if she hadn't been hoping to see Jimmy at the fair, she'd have run after Rose and begged her to take them home with her. But she couldn't stop thinking about that night Jimmy gave her the pink pendant, fastened it gently around her neck and kissed her sweetly on the lips.

So she patted the wave Aunt Rose had formed so carefully on the side of her face. And soon as Rose had disappeared into the stone station, she jumped down from the cart and lifted her arms to help Cyrus down. She was hungry, they had to eat something first. Those nice blue boxes of Rice Krispies tempted her greatly, but Pa was distracted, already stepping out to cross the street toward the Cascade Tavern.

Just then, Bonnie heard the ah-ooh-gah of a horn and saw a black sedan rush past them. Pa looked back toward the cart, swearing.

"Was that Mama?" Cyrus cried. He'd run out into the middle of the road now, too, standing feet wide apart, chubby little arms waving above his head.

Bonnie and Pa exchanged a look but no words

"Come on, Cyrus. We gotta go. Now," she said. She pointed toward a gigantic red wheel that soared over the fairground, rotating as Bonnie watched. "Ferris Wheel," she told Cyrus. "That's where we're headed." Then, blinking, she reached out tentatively to touch Pa's arm. "You said we could go. You promised Aunt Rose."

"Did no such thing. Not one to make promises like that."

"But she told us." Bonnie bit her lip so hard she recognized the coppery taste of blood.

Across the street at the tavern, a man in denim pants and a chore jacket had been leaning against one of its three white pillars. He tipped the brim of his cap at Pa.

"We don't need you to come with us," she said quickly. "You can enjoy yourself here in town." She wouldn't want Pa around when she saw Jimmy anyway.

Pa hesitated, still looking at the Tavern. "Well, I might as well have a beer or two."

Bonnie knew those would turn into five or six.

"We need money for the tickets,." The blood she could still taste on her lip was keeping her steady. Pa was a mystery, and she never knew what would set him off.

"Can we have some money for tickets then, Pa?" Cyrus asked. Those big blue eyes staring up at the tall figure of the father.

"Aw, dammit, Cyrus," Pa said.

"Mama said not to…" Bonnie started then stopped. Mama didn't like them swearing, didn't want Cyrus picking up bad habits.

Cyrus little fingers were wrapped together like he held them saying his prayers at night when Mama had been the one to tuck them in. There'd be no tucking in now that Rose was gone, at least not til Mama came back.

"Please?" Cyrus said, and Bonnie held her breath.

The man in the work jacket had disappeared inside the tavern. Pa sighed. "All right then," he said and pulled a rumpled bill from his pocket. "Here," he said to Bonnie.

"Thank you," she said and pulled Cyrus away before Pa wanted the money back. As Pa started to cross the road again, after being sure no cars were racing past, Bonnie and Cyrus walked quickly down the street in the direction of the fairgrounds. Dirt coated their bare feet. In front of the post office, two boys were playing a game, using sticks for guns. They stopped to wave the sticks at Cyrus. A "Work Pays America" poster hung on the brick wall behind them.

Finally they reached the entry gate to the fairgrounds. Beyond the gate, Bonnie could see large gun-gray metal buildings and fenced outdoor pens holding cows, pigs, sheep. Off to the side a small car raced around an oval track; cheers rang from the grandstand. There were three rows of white stands with awnings. Carnival games and spinning cotton candy machines. Popcorn makers and a red, yellow, and white midway wheel. And towering over it all, that amazing red Ferris wheel.

Bonnie smoothed the dollar bill Pa had given her and gave it to a man in a red-and-white striped shirt handing out tickets. "Two, please."

She stuck the tickets and the leftover change in a tie-circle pocket at the front of her dress then reached up to make sure her necklace was centered in the hollow of her neck.

"Jimmy Steadman may be here," she whispered to Cyrus. "Remember, he's the one that gave me this necklace."

"Jimmy Jo, Jimmy Jo, Jimmy Jo. Bonnie's got a boyfriend."

She shook her head. "I don't know. I haven't seen him since Mama went away. But I hope so."

Cyrus wasn't interested. He pulled on her arm. "Carousel! Carousel!"

Bonnie had wanted to go to the 4-H exhibits first, knowing that's where Jimmy would probably be. But Cyrus would whine, so she took him by the hand toward a beautiful round carousel. Loud whistles came from a music roll looping through a red, blue, and yellow calliope, and a man sat in the middle whittling a small horse.

Bonnie set Cyrus up on a saddled ostrich, and then she chose a white horse with gold mane, tail, and hooves for herself. On the third rotation, she caught the brass ring that entitled her to another ride. She held the free ticket for a long time before giving it to Cyrus and then stood watching him go around and around, this time on a striped tiger, a knot of resentment in her stomach. If Mama were here, Bonnie could head to the 4-H exhibits now, not be stuck with her little brother.

"I'm hungry," he said when he climbed down.

Bonnie found a concession stand where she bought two corn dogs. They sat on a bench beside the racetrack to eat. She kept an eye on the crowd, in case Jimmy wandered past.

"Wonder what Mama's doing now," Cyrus said.

When Bonnie didn't answer, Cyrus shrugged and took another bite of his corn dog. Ketchup dribbled down his chin, and Bonnie wiped it off with her finger.

Bonnie thought about the "women's problems" Pa had said he didn't have time for. Back in April, Mama complained of stomach cramps and took to bed, losing the baby that would have been her and Cyrus's new little brother or sister, Bonnie wasn't sure, even though she'd seen the poor thing, like a little piece of raw liver, dark and shiny with something that looked like a kidney bean inside. Pa scooped it into a ball of crumpled newspaper and took it away while Mama wept.

After that, Mama was sad. She wore the same clothes days in a row and stopped doing chores. Nobody liked it when Pa yelled, so Bonnie took on additional tasks, sweeping the floors, straining the morning's milk, and on wash day, pouring the heavy tubful of heated water into the machine. She had to jump down on the crank to get it going.

Cyrus tapped Bonnie's knee.

"What?" she said, startled. Then, "Come on, let's go see the cows and chickens."

Cyrus' face crumpled, and she felt bad so she said, "Ferris wheel first. Race you."

Bonnie took a fast start but slowed down to let Cyrus catch up as they neared the towering ride. A man in a plaid shirt locked them into a car, and Cyrus held Bonnie's hand as they started to go up. After four full turns, the ride stopped as people were let off below. Bonnie and Cyrus were stuck near the top.

"Can you see our house, Bonnie? Can you see where Mama is?"

"Not from here, silly. But see how tiny everybody is. And the cars. They're like toys." She'd never seen the world from up so high. It was like spinning the large knob on the microscope all the way right and adjusting the small knob so even though things were far away, amazing details could be seen.

"It's like one of Mama's quilts, isn't it, Cyrus?" Red barns and dirt roads, a thin blue river snaking through.

When it was their turn to get off, the man in the plaid shirt lifted the latch and helped them onto the platform.

"I'm glad Pa's not here yet," Cyrus said as they headed to the exhibition hall.

"Me too." She hoped Pa wouldn't be drunk when he did show up.

As if reading her thoughts, Cyrus said, "Frank Haggerty showed me how to make the foam go down in a glass of beer."

"How?"

"You stick two fingers in it."

Bonnie shook her head. "You shouldn't be talking about beer in third grade. I ought to tell Mrs. Haggerty." She thought this is what Mama would have done.

"Don't, Bonnie! Promise you won't."

"I won't."

Near the entrance to the exhibition hall, women sat at card tables selling home-made pickles, jams, crocheted doilies. It was noisy; voices echoed off the metal walls and ceilings.

Bonnie saw Jimmy Steadman standing by a horse stall. He wore a red-and-black checked shirt and dark blue jeans.

"Quiet!" she said to Cyrus.

"I didn't say anything!"

"Well, don't. And stay here. I'll be back."

"Stay where?"

"Here," she said, pushing him toward a girl with glasses who was brushing a pet rabbit.

She looked to see if Jimmy was still near the stall and then hurried over to a shiny new car parked in the middle aisle. A sign in its window read: FOR SALE, $700, NO LESS BUT HAPPY TO TAKE MORE. A man was bent over, checking the tires, while his wife reached into an open window to touch the leather seat.

Bonnie glanced into the side mirror. A thermometer ran down its edge: 96 degrees. Her straw-yellow hair fell flat on her head, her skin was pasty white, and a drop of Cyrus' ketchup stained her dress. She mussed her hair, took a deep breath, and walked around the car to the stall where Jimmy was. A blue ribbon with a fancy rosette hung from the stall door.

"Hey," she said, fingering the stiff satin of the ribbon. "Congratulations."

"Thanks." Jimmy always won ribbons at 4-H shows. He was a poor student, which is why she'd helped him with homework. He'd been so grateful and then after Mama's baby came out too early and died, he'd made her a necklace from a piece of broken glass. He'd fastened it around her neck as they sat on her front porch, giving her a quick kiss on the cheek.

"What did you and Chester win for?"

"Two-forty trot and the sulky." His eyes were like astonishing green marbles.

"You know Old Man Wheeler?" Jimmy said. "From Parkins? Nearly got himself killed this morning. He was behind me in the race so I didn't see it happen, but I heard about it after from Marlene."

Bonnie flinched.

"Marlene said Wheeler pulled out to pass someone, and his horse's hoof caught on the wheel of John Burns' sulky. He got thrown against the rail."

Jimmy was stroking Chester's withers, ignoring her.

"What happened to him?" Bonnie asked.

"They took him to the hospital. Haven't heard any more than that."

"Oh."

Before Bonnie could think of something else to say, Jimmy grinned and waved at someone. Three someones: Marlene, Rose, and Edith. Marlene in a navy sailor dress with white collar and bow, Edith in a bright red jumper, and Rose in a fancy buckram hat. Bonnie thought they looked ready for a shopping trip to Kansas City, not for a County Fair.

Marlene raised her eyebrows and gave Bonnie a fake smile.

Another horse was being led into the stall next to Chester's.

"That's the horse that got hurt," Jimmy said.

"What will they do with him?" Bonnie asked though she knew as well as any of them.

"Shoot him," Rose said. "He won't be good for anything now."

"But can't someone just take care of him?"

Marlene laughed at Bonnie, fingering a thin gold chain that dropped into the collar of her sailor dress. "Nobody wants a horse that can't race or work. You of all people should know that, considering what your Pa did."

Jimmy stood with his hands in his pockets, studying the dirt floor of the exhibition hall.

"I have to find my brother," Bonnie said, turning her back on all of them.

Cyrus wasn't standing where she'd left him, and the girl with the rabbit was gone.

She hurried out of the hall. The crowd was thicker now and the sky darker.

"Cyrus!" she yelled again and again until finally he answered in his sweet voice. She found him with the two boys they'd seen playing in front of the post office that morning. The boys had joined an egg toss behind one of the concession stands.

Bonnie grabbed a paper cup filled with ice water and watched Cyrus toss his egg, which broke in the grass, spilling a yellow sphere and cloudy liquid, that made her think of the thing that had come from inside Mama.

She felt a raindrop on her arm.

"I want another chance!" Cyrus huffed.

Marlene was walking arm-in-arm with Edith and Rose toward the egg toss.

"We've got to find Pa," Bonnie said.

But Marlene had stepped up beside Bonnie, and the woman in charge of the toss handed them each an egg. "Your turn soon, girls."

"Your mama still sent away?" Marlene asked.

Bonnie stared at the curls framing Marlene's face and then toward the Ferris wheel rimmed with white lights.

"She wasn't sent away," Bonnie said. The girls surrounded her, and Jimmy had joined them.

"My mother told me what happened," Marlene said, winking at Jimmy.

Bonnie bit her lip. "She's at the hospital. That's all."

"Hospital in St. Joe?" Jimmy grinned, and Bonnie's stomach turned.

She didn't know which hospital. Pa hadn't told her, and she'd been afraid to ask. "I guess so." She felt the egg cradled in her hand.

"Well," Jimmy said. "You're smart. You must know what kind of hospital that is."

Bonnie blinked. She did know but tried hard to pretend she didn't, just like she'd done with the injured horse.

"State Asylum #2," Rose said in a sing-song.

"Pa's waiting for me and Cyrus," Bonnie said, but the others didn't budge.

She kept waiting for Jimmy to speak up, come to her rescue. He'd been so kind that evening on the porch, after Bonnie had told him about her mother's loss of the baby.

Marlene took a step closer. Raindrops had stained the girl's starched navy sailor dress.

"State Asylum Number Two is where they put crazy people," Marlene said. "I heard your father had your Mama committed there." Marlene adjusted a red ribbon in her hair. "Maybe she'll have shock treatment. A man over in Marshall got sent there for killing his brother. They gave him shock treatments twice a week." She turned as though she were telling the story to Jimmy, but kept her eyes locked on Bonnie's. "They put a piece of rubber in his mouth to keep him from chewing his tongue off."

To Bonnie's horror, Jimmy laughed.

Marlene reached down the front of her dress and pulled out a pendant of pink glass just like Bonnie's.

Without thinking, Bonnie threw the egg in her hand at Marlene. It broke on one of the dress's shiny brass buttons. Thick clear and yellow liquid spread down the front of the navy fabric.

"What did you do that for?" Marlene shouted.

Bonnie pushed past them all and grabbed Cyrus.

It started raining harder as they moved toward the entrance gate. People covered their heads with newspapers and took shelter under awnings.

"There he is." Cyrus pointed toward Pa, leaning against the fence that surrounded the fairgrounds.

The rain made it hard to see clearly, but Bonnie could make out a can in his hand.

She closed her eyes and wished that when she opened them, everything would be different.

She wanted to be back up on the Ferris wheel, in a car at the very top, with everyone else—except Mama and Aunt Rose and maybe Cyrus—down below, small and insignificant. She wanted to turn whatever knobs there were on the world so the sight of Mama's terrified face in the back of that black car would disappear.

But mostly, she wanted everything to stop so she wouldn't have to take Mama's place doing extra chores at home and so no man, not Pa, not Jimmy, none of them, could have any say at all about anything inside her.

"Farmer's Daughter" by Thomas Hart Benton

THE SWEET PERFUME OF
SOMEWHERE ELSE

Missouri, 1944

It hadn't rained in weeks, and we were desperate for something, anything, to break the heat. The corn had shriveled up, and Pa said that morning that if the rains don't come soon, come fall we'll have nothing to sell and nothing to eat.

He'd brought in as much of the crop as he could for silage, then borrowed a bucket scraper from the state Conservation Commission program to start digging a pond in the back fields, to collect whatever rain might one day come. He worked from dawn to dusk, leaving

Charlie and me in charge of all the house and farm chores Mama used to do.

One morning near the end of August, I caught Pa before he left for the day.

"There's a 4-H club meeting this afternoon. Can Charlie and I go?"

Before Mama died, Pa had been happy. Now his face was like stone, and I worried that even the pressure of my words hanging in the air between us might bring him pain. But he lifted his shoulders a quarter of an inch and let them fall. I took that as a Yes.

So I packed two lunch pails with buttered cornbread, pimento ham, and graham crackers. Then I whistled for Sonny Boy, our sweet, flat-headed mutt, and he followed me outside as I stepped, one-two-three-four, from stone to stone, then climbed on the wooden platform that held the pump. Pa had left a low trough there after warning me not to take any more water than needed.

A hot wind pressed the thin cotton of my dress against my bare stomach and legs as I reached for the cast-iron handle. I'd taken extra pains dressing that day and pinned my 4-H pin—a four-leaf clover with letters that stood for Head, Heart, Hands, and Health—carefully above where I hoped a breast would one day be.

The pump's inner workings clanged but no water came out. I kept pumping up-down, up-down. Nothing. Pa had left a hoe tilting against the front of the house. There was a trap door to the root cellar where we'd hidden last summer when a tornado ripped through town. I remembered sitting on Mama's lap down there and her singing songs to keep me and Charlie calm: "Star Dust" and "Swinging on a Star," "Peg O'My Heart"—songs she'd sung at a club in Chicago before she'd married Pa and left the big city for a small Missouri farm.

Sonny Boy's ears were pressed back against his head. Behind him the sky was streaked with dull gray clouds. I needed the weather and everything about my life to change. There was something important I had to do, something that scared what Charlie would call the bejesus out of me.

The new county agent for 4-H had insisted we keep meeting despite the months-long drought. His name was Billy Pendergast, and he resembled Gary Cooper, with a delicate mouth, light-brown hair, and blue eyes. I'd tacked a picture of the movie star, torn from the cover of *Screen Romance*, to the wall in my bedroom.

Mr. Prendergast—*Call me Billy*—hadn't been in town long before somebody asked him to take over after our last club leader moved away. Nobody knew much about the newcomer except that he'd come from Chicago and had maybe been a teacher there. Charlie and I figured Mrs. Baxeter was the one who had roped him into taking care of our 4-H club because she was so pretty she was able to talk anybody into doing anything.

Mrs. Baxeter was the mother of my best friend, Julie. In her bedroom she had a dressing table covered with jewelry—clip earrings and choker necklaces—and half a dozen perfume bottles in clear and blue glass, frosted crystal, and white enamel. Last week I'd sat at this dressing table with Julie while her mother was downstairs, cooking broiled chicken and cabbage salad for supper.

"He's handsome, isn't he?" I said.

"Who?" Julie was pulling something from a pocket of her cuffed shorts. "I borrowed this," she said, holding out a black bottle with a black lid. "Bandit. Eau de toilette."

When I didn't reach for it, Julie unscrewed the lid, then held the open bottle under my nose. I smelled leather, maybe smoke.

"Mr. Pendergast, silly." Even saying his name sent a shiver through me.

She tipped the bottle, wetting her index finger and rubbing the perfume onto her wrist and inner elbow.

Then the scent hit me harder, dark and intense, but with something underneath, something sweet.

"How old do you think he is?" I asked.

I couldn't tell if she was wrinkling her nose because she didn't like the smell of the perfume or because she didn't like Mr. P.

"Early thirties," she said, standing up and bringing her wrist to her nose, inhaling deeply.

So it was Mr. P. she didn't like. But I did. I chewed my lip and pressed on. "So why isn't he married?"

"Exactly. And why'd he leave Chicago if it's so great?" She pulled a piece of Bazooka Bubble Gum from her other pocket, removed the red, white, and blue wrapper, and tore the gum in two, handing me half. "That man gives me the creeps, Cherise."

I was confused because I'd seen how Mr. Pendergast always paid extra attention to Julie during our club meetings. We'd met about four times since he came to town, always in a back room at the schoolhouse. He'd announced at our first meeting that the National 4-H Camp would meet in Chicago this year and that our small district in Missouri had one representative slot left to fill. He'd handed out applications at the second meeting, and both Julie and I took one.

We'd all heard how the McGinty twins' older brother had gone to the National 4-H Camp in 1941, the year before he'd been shipped overseas. He'd slept in a tent at the base of the Washington Monument. Missouri had never sent a girl to represent the state, but I was bound and determined to be the first, if I could figure out how to get Mr. Pendergast to choose my application over the others. I absolutely had to be chosen.

I hadn't told Papa I had applied, but Charlie was in on my secret. And he was just as set as I was on getting me there.

"I can see where Mama met Papa," I told him. "I can see the clubs where she sang. And I can ask Grandpa and Grandma Hickok for help for Pa."

I knew my mama's parents were rich, though I'd never met them. They'd been so angry when she ran off with a poor farmer, they refused to have anything more to do with her. Mama had told me stories about the street she grew up on in Lincoln Park and the house with its thick carpets and sparkling chandeliers. I thought maybe I could persuade them to at least give Pa the loan he hadn't been able to get from the bank. I'd heard him tell Julie's father that pretty much all our savings had gone to pay Mama's doctors.

The first hurdle, of course, was getting to Chicago by persuading Mr. Pendergast to choose me over Julie. He did seem to like her better. During our last meeting, our third, he'd caught Julie's arm as she walked past his chair. Her feet, in white anklets and black Mary Janes, flew up in the air as he pulled her to sit on his lap. She laughed but jumped off and ran back to the table where Charlie and I, Ralph Adams, and the McGinty twins sat counting the money we'd raised that week selling war bonds and rags and scrap iron.

It didn't feel good to be jealous of my best friend. But somehow I had to find a way to be picked.

Mama had always told me I was pretty. But I was skinny, and now that Papa was the one cutting my hair, I was sometimes mistaken for a boy. My arms were bony and my hands too big at the end of them. And I was shy. Charlie called me Mouse.

Last summer, before Mama got so sick, she'd taken Charlie and me to a dance at church one Sunday afternoon. She'd showed us how to jitterbug and do the lindy, singing along with the little band they had there. She'd tied my hair, still long, with a pretty, powder-blue satin ribbon to match the gingham dress she'd sewed for me. She'd even pinned a little silver posey to hold my skirt up for dancing. But I spent the evening sitting by myself on a bench at the back of the church hall.

I knew that Mama would have asked lots of questions when Mr. Pendergast was invited to be our new 4-H club leader. She would have wanted to know more about where he'd taught in Chicago, where he'd lived.

But she'd been dead two months when he came to town so mysteriously, and Pa had his hands full with the farm and with his grief. Charlie and I did whatever we could to help with chores, but it never seemed to be enough. Pa was always busy and mostly stayed away from us, working outside all day and sitting in his chair without talking at night after supper.

So when Mr. Pendergast came, nobody questioned him much, and he started holding meetings every other week at the schoolhouse. He told us he had a cousin fighting in the war, though he couldn't remember exactly where. The first meeting he'd handed out little blue books with lined paper where we could keep track of our pledge to "raise food for fighters." If we did well, he promised, he'd pick one of us to go to the Camp.

I'll go with whoever goes, he'd told us. *You can assure your parents you'll be safe.*

I'd figured Julie had the better chance of being picked.

But when Pa said that about not having any food to eat come fall, I knew I had to do something fast. So after I washed the breakfast dishes with the trickle of water I managed to get out of the pump, and let Sonny Boy have a secret drink, I gave my short hair an extra brushing and ran back upstairs into Pa's bedroom, the one he'd shared with Mama.

Mama had never been one to wear makeup or perfume like Julie's mother did, but I remembered seeing a green floral tin of talcum powder, Emeraude by Coty, that she'd kept in the medicine cabinet between the mercury thermometer and a bottle of iodine with a skull and crossbones on the label. In the four months since Mama had died, Pa hadn't gotten rid of any of her things, so I found the tin quickly, pulled off the top, and immediately swooned in the lemon and orange scent of love.

I missed my mama desperately. I hadn't cried once since the funeral, not once. Papa wasn't crying so I figured I shouldn't either; I had to be strong for him.

It was always a relief not to have Pa around during the long hours he was up in the back field digging out the pond. There was this huge heaviness whenever he was in the house with us. Sometimes I wanted to tie strings to his shoulders and lift them like a puppet's, lift them high at the wonder of the world I kept trying to tell myself surely must still be found somewhere.

I got to the 4-H club meeting early. When I walked in, the room was empty, and I put the two lunch pails inside a closet on a low shelf. I pulled out the green tin of talcum I'd tucked inside one of the pails and poured some white powder on a puff I'd found below the sink in the bathroom. It smelled like Mama and love, too, and remembering Julie's gestures with her mama's eau de toilette, I dabbed the puff inside both wrists and the hollow of my neck. A cloud of white dust rose up around me.

Because of the glass that made up the top half of the door, I could see Mr. Pendergast before he walked into the classroom. Despite the heat he wore a long-sleeve shirt buttoned at the collar, pressed jeans with a leather belt.

"Meeting doesn't start for half an hour, Cherise," he said with a frown. "Wait outside, why don't you?"

I started to head toward the door, but I caught a glimpse of the dry grass outside the window, burned to a crisp by the drought, and I thought how awful it would be to see Papa sitting so sad again that night, and about what he'd said about us not having food next fall if the rain didn't come. I thought about Chicago and the Hickoks in Lincoln Park with their fancy house. They were my blood relatives, and surely they'd help Pa if they knew how much he needed it. Grandma Hickok had even sent a note to Charlie and me after Mama's funeral. It was formal and Pa said it was mean and cold, but still, it was a note.

So I stepped out of the closet and walked toward Mr. P.

I thought that if he wasn't so handsome, what I had to do might be easier.

I thought back to the dance Mama had taken us to, remembering how Julie and the other girls had had plenty of boys lined up to dance with them. It was something they did, something about the way they held their mouths or blinked their eyes.

"Billy." I couldn't believe what I'd just said. But he'd told us to call him by his first name, told us that on our very first meeting with him. My mouth was dry and it was hard to talk, but I pressed on. "I have a question about my application to Camp."

"It's fine," he said.

Standing there, with the scent of Emeraude, of Mama, cocooning both of us, I tried to imagine myself pretty. I tried to pretend I was someone a boy, a man, would want to dance with. Hold in his arms. Do anything for.

I was standing so close to Mr. P. that I could smell a scent coming off him as well, urgent and metallic and wrong. I saw that there were half-moons of sweat in the armpits of his shirt. It was as though putting on Mama's powder had heightened my senses, like Superman in Charlie's comics.

Maybe Mr. Pendergast had something like x-ray vision too, or could read my mind, because he took two quick steps toward me and put both hands on my shoulders, pulling me toward him.

I squirmed out of his hold and ran back into the closet where I'd left my blue notebook. I waved it in his face like a weapon.

"I want to go to Chicago," I said. "I wrote another essay, and I want you to read it."

He smiled but it wasn't a real smile.

"You want to go to Chicago," he said, slowly repeating my words. "Yes."

The blue notebook shook in my outstretched hand. I could almost see a dirty movie rolling in his head as he stood there, staring at me, running his eyes up and down the front of my dress. I could feel those eyes touch my skin through the thin cotton and then his hand below the 4-H pin I'd placed so carefully that morning.

And then a shadow darkened the glass of the door, and the door opened, and Julie and Charlie walked in. Julie raised her eyebrows and, without saying a word, Mr. Prendergast left the room.

Later, when we were walking home, Charlie said he'd never seen me so frightened. He didn't ask why I smelled to high heaven of Mama's Emeraude or say much of anything else. It had started raining and both the rain and his silence felt like enormous gifts.

When we got to the farm, we ran out to the back field, Sonny Boy chasing after us, his reddish-brown hair darkened in the rain. His little ears flapped happily as we ran. We found Pa standing by the pond he'd been working so hard to dig. He was just standing there, his arms raised toward the dark sky, watching raindrops stream down from it and land silently on the cracked red clay in the empty hole. His hair, too, lay wet and dark against his head and when he turned and saw us, I thought there were tears streaming down his face mixed in with the rain. The backhoe loomed large behind him, rain streaking down its sides and cleaning the yellow cab and huge tires of the dry, caked dirt that had accumulated all that long, hot summer. Charlie and I went up to Pa and wrapped our arms around him, and the three of us stood there, walking in a slow circle like a prayer.

At that moment I wanted to stay twelve years old as long as I could. I knew the world was about to become a scarier place, even if it rained for days and even if I never traveled far from home. There were three of us in the circle now, not four, and finally I let my own tears fall and slip into the baked and thirsty earth.

"The Prodigal Son" by Thomas Hart Benton

PRODIGAL SON

The first time Alvin met Owney Madden, he'd been charmed. Madden was strikingly handsome, in a way even other men can admire. It was New Year's Eve, 1924. Alvin was 18 years old, had recently run away from home, and was working as a bartender at the Arlington Hotel in Hot Springs, Arkansas. There was a dinner dance that night, in the Crystal Ballroom. Most of the crowd was on the dance floor or eating at cloth-topped tables while black-vested waiters carried drinks garnished with pink stirrers and corkscrews of lemon rinds.

Alvin was drying the footplate of a cocktail glass with a white towel when the man approached. Blue-black hair, a hawk nose, everything about him perfect and whole.

"Ever been to New York City?" The man leaned on the mahogany bar. Diamond cufflinks sparkled at his wrists.

"Can't say I have," Alvin said. "This here's my first time out of Piney Grove."

A pretty short-haired blonde in a blue sequined dress laid her hand on the man's shoulder, but he shook his head. She pouted then walked away.

"You feel familiar," he said to Alvin. "Thought I might have met you back in the city."

"Nope. Never been." Alvin closed his eyes for a moment, picturing the farm where he'd grown up: a small but neatly-cared for house on a narrow dirt road; a silo; the few cows, horses, pigs; the thresher that had maimed his father and left him incomplete. Alvin cleared his throat loudly, trying to sound like a man rather than the boy he was. All that was behind him, he told himself. Hot Springs would be a fresh start.

"Hey," the man said. When Alvin opened his eyes, he saw that the man held out one large hand, smooth with well-tended nails. "Name's Owen Madden. My friends call me Owney."

A grin crawled up one side of the man's face as he saw recognition dawn on Alvin's face. "Son, you don't know the half of it," he said. "Say, you know how to make a South Side Fizz? Favored drink of Al and his crew up in Chicago."

Alvin swallowed and busied himself wiping the towel in circles on the top of the bar. "'Fraid I don't."

"Gin. Lemon Juice. Club Soda. Mint. Syrup. Hold the ginger ale."

"Yes, sir," Alvin said, his voice cracking. It was only when he turned away from the man to make the drink that he exhaled.

"Everything go all right tonight, honey?" Marlena asked when he finally crawled into bed later that night. They'd found a room in a boarding house; Marlena—or her pretty face and figure—had persuaded the owner to let them stay for free in exchange for her cooking and cleaning.

She lay in their narrow bed, one arm over her eyes, but Alvin pulled it away and bent down to kiss her, slipping his fingers under the straps of her gown. They'd gone to school together back in Piney Grove. Taken the four-hour bus ride together from there to Hot Springs. Stood before a carrot-haired justice of the peace in a small building with an old Sears washing machine on its front porch. His mother sent a set of hand-embroidered pillowcases as a wedding gift. They lay in a white box on top of the dresser, next to a bottle of cheap wine.

"Mmm-hhh," Alvin said, laughing. He could smell the wine on Marlena's breath. "Yes, everything went well."

Owen—Owney—Madden was 40 years old and also a newcomer to Hot Springs. He sat talking to Alvin Parsons for two hours that night in the Crystal Ballroom of the Arlington Hotel, ignoring the women in ball gowns and men in tuxedos, the sparkling glasses of champagne being served on gleaming trays of silver. When midnight struck, Madden and Parsons clicked glasses; they had a deal.

Alvin lay next to Marlena in his boxers and snuggled his body against hers.

"Good tips?" Marlena asked, pulling his hand away from between her legs and resting it firmly on her stomach. "I'm sleepy, darlin'. It's late."

So he didn't tell her about the handsome, generous man he'd met, the one who'd been written up in all the papers last year when he was released from Sing-Sing after serving nine of a 20-year sentence for the murder of Little Patsy Doyle. Madden had assured Alvin all that was behind him now that he'd come to Arkansas for a quiet life. But money was to be made if young Alvin was smart enough to see it.

He lay there in bed, unable to sleep. He hadn't admitted to Marlena how scared he had been, wondering if they could actually make it on their own once they left Piney Grove. But now that he'd met Mr. Madden, everything would be fine. Nothing had been fine back on the farm, least of all his father.

Roy Parsons had lost his hands in a threshing accident two years earlier. His hands and forearms were caught in the remorseless grip of a threshing machine; his bones were pulled from their sockets and instantly shattered.

Most summers, the day the community thresher came was a great occasion. Three or four men travelled with the machine from farm to farm, and all the neighbors gathered to pitch in. Alvin's mother was busy in the kitchen with the other women that morning, making fried chicken, biscuits, and gravy for the noonday meal.

Roy acted as feeder, shoving the grain into the cylinder of the thresher. All morning he'd stood there amidst the clattering noise and dust and turmoil, tall, straight, and blue-eyed.

Alvin's job was to tend the blower, direct the already-threshed grain onto a cart pulled by a team of horses. It was a dusty, sweaty job but one that, at least when he was younger, he'd been happy to have. That summer, though, as he turned sixteen, his mind turned elsewhere, and on that particular day was filled with thoughts of Marlena Hinkle, a new girl who'd just moved to Piney Grove.

"Hurry up, boy!" Roy had shouted at Eugene Newcomb, a boy from Alvin's school. "Get your lazy ass up here with that cart." Eugene sneered, annoyed, but pulled the cart alongside a twisted rubber belt connecting the thresher to a steam engine. Then he let the reins to the horses drop to his lap.

One of the team reared back on its hind legs, and both animals galloped forward. Their sudden movement pulled Alvin out of his dreamy reverie about Marlena and made Roy turn to see what had happened. That moment's lapse on Roy's part saw both his hands and forearms caught in the wicked teeth and half-moon blades of the machine.

His father bent at an odd angle into the maw of the thresher. It was only when Alvin reached his side that he realized how much blood there was. The teeth of the thresher were still turning, and tatters of his father's denim blue workshirt spun around. Finally someone, Alvin never knew who, turned off the engine, and when the terrible noise of the machine had stopped, Roy let out a single, low guttural moan. Then silence.

"Oh god, oh god, oh god," Alvin said.

Two men, neighbors, helped pull what was left of Roy's arms out. When Alvin saw those shapeless blobs, he vomited over the side of the platform. Below him on the ground, he saw his father's flesh, ground to a pulp and dotted with grain that sparkled in the noonday sun.

Somehow they wrapped the ends of Roy's arms in a ripped shirt and helped him back to the house. Somebody knocked over a yellow ware bowl that held the pieces of chicken Mama had bathed overnight in buttermilk. Cut-up thighs, breasts, legs—skin all puckered—slid onto the floor, surrounded by bits of pottery.

Roy, who hadn't said a word, walked without speaking into the bathroom and climbed into the claw-footed bathtub where he removed the bloodied fabric and sat there.

"So the blood don't get on the floor," he said before he passed out.

It was thought for days that Roy would die from shock and loss of blood.

But Doc Newcomb, Eugene's father, was able to amputate both arms below the elbow, and after the furrowed scars left on the stubs had healed, fitted Roy with prostheses. The leather bent at the elbows, and the hooks were positioned at the ends of iron wrist-pieces and had pincers.

Those first weeks back home, Roy would wake at 4:30 in the morning, like always, and haul Alvin out of bed. He'd make his son help him strap on the reddish-brown leather. Roy's eyes brimmed with tears each time, and Alvin, because he couldn't face his father's fear, grew angry.

That first month, Alvin followed his father outside for their regular chores: turning the stock into the pastures, leading the horses to a nearby spring, carrying pails of swill to the hogs. The one thing Roy couldn't do was milk the cows' tender udders.

One morning, Roy and Alvin sat eating breakfast in the kitchen. A spray of bride's wreath stood in a jelly jar in the center of the table, and Mama cooked at the stove with her back to them.

Roy grabbed a link of sausage between the pincers, steering it toward his mouth. Grits were harder. Doc Newcomb said there was a contraption that could tie a spoon to the end of the prosthesis, but sometimes Roy got impatient, just bent down low toward the plate and pushed the food up into his mouth with his hook.

It made Alvin sick to his stomach to watch him.

"Marlena asked me to go to the circus in Midway tomorrow." He spoke down into his dinner plate. Marlena Hinkle had been particularly friendly to Alvin since the accident.

"Nope. We've got work to do," Roy said.

Alvin had never minded doing chores before, but that summer, the thought of being stuck on the farm for the rest of his life, strapping and unstrapping his father's prostheses, and having to see those dreadful hooks every day, was more than he could bear.

"I'd like to go to the circus," he said quietly.

Roy reached across the table and took one split hook to Alvin's cheek. Alvin could feel the two blades pressing into his skin.

He yelled, and Mama shouted out, "Roy, stop that!" She wiped her own hands frantically on her white pinafore apron.

Before she could reach them, Alvin had pushed his chair back. He stayed away from the farm all that day and the next. When he snuck back in late Saturday night, Mama was in a rocking chair waiting up for him. He handed her a ruby red shot glass he'd won at a Penny Pitch game and went to bed without saying a word.

The next morning, he told his mother that Marlena Hinkle's father had friends in Hot Springs who would hire him for work. This was a lie, and she probably knew it but said nothing. He told her he couldn't stay on the farm any longer. She left the room and returned carrying a tan rattan suitcase.

"This is what I used when I moved here from Chicago," she said.

Owney Madden brought Alvin into the liquor business and set him and Marlena up in a nice suite at the Arlington Hotel.

"No cleaning other peoples' rooms for you, pretty lady," Owney said.

"Thank you, Mr. Madden," Marlena answered, blushing. Both

Alvin and Marlena called him Mr. Madden those first weeks, but soon it was Owney.

"People don't come here to have a nice, leisurely drink," Owney said one evening three years later as they sat at the bar at his new casino, the Southern Club. "They come to guzzle alcohol while they can."

Marlene giggled and sipped her sidecar. She now wore heavy makeup and low-cut blouses, looked nothing like the farm girl Alvin had married. Owney always said how gorgeous she looked, but Alvin preferred the earlier version.

Owney had brought in Alvin as Director of Operations for the casino, implied this would set the young man up for life. He taught Alvin how to skim a little extra on the side, too: rigging deals with blackjack players so they'd have a lucky streak and share their winnings, slipping in a pre-loaded deck.

"Your Dad drink as much as mine did?" Owney played with an unlit cigarette.

Alvin shook his head.

He'd never figured out why Owney took him under his wing. Might be because Owney had run away from home young, too. He'd told Alvin about his dad being a petty thief, growing up in Hell's Kitchen, joining a gang called the Gophers.

"Irish are my family," Madden said. "Not those devils I was born to."

Once, when Alvin told Owney about his father's accident, about losing his hands, he admitted that sometimes he felt guilty. Like it might have been his fault. His mother had sent him letters through the years, telling him how Pa could now button his shirts by himself, even prepare a cigarette. She'd asked him to take over the farm, prayed he would come home. But every time Alvin thought of those black hooks, he cringed.

"Just bad, bad luck, that's what most would call it," Owney had said. "Me, I don't buy into that. Ain't nothing lucky or unlucky about it. Life happens. My piece of advice to you is: Make your own way."

Then he'd taken Alvin outside to show him his new Studebaker Champion. Top of the line. Color of sweet cream. Alvin was sitting on the leather upholstery in that car when Owney pushed the gun onto his palm. "Colt Vest Pocket," Owney had said. "Great for unobtrusive carry."

Alvin didn't tell his boss that he'd never shot a thing other than a rabbit when he was ten. The bunny had thrown a somersault when the bullet hit and let out a high-pitched scream.

Alvin had been at the Southern Casino for ten years when he got the news his mother had died. He wanted to go home for the funeral, but there was a big shipment of liquor due, and Owney insisted Alvin be there himself to oversee it. "Make sure nobody skims off the top. And take that gun with you, Parsons." But then a few months later the letter from The Pike County Bank and Trust arrived.

"I've got to go home," he said to Marlena. She had her back to him, waiting for him to pull up the zipper on the new dress she'd bought. It was silver-gray and beaded, with gray fringe at the knees. They were due to go dancing at the casino that night.

"Zip me up, sweetcakes." Her words slurred, and she lifted a glass half-filled with whiskey.

"This is important," he said, taking her face in both hands.

"Nothing's important in Piney Grove," she said. "Don't you remember?"

"The farm's in foreclosure," he said. "Pa's going to be evicted if I don't get there to help."

She pulled away from him, stumbled out the door. "Then I'll just mosey downstairs and have a drinkie-poo myself. Owney'll take care of me," she said.

Two days later, standing on the narrow dirt road that led to the farm, Alvin lowered the old rattan suitcase, the one his mother had given him. It was held together now by two coils of rope in addition to its rusted locks. He stared at the hodge-podge of crazily tilted boards and cracked shingles that had been his childhood home.

Somewhere behind those boarded-up windows, his father would be stewing in the late August heat.

Alvin rubbed his beard, gone prematurely gray in the last year.

He stared at the skeleton of a cow, its bleached bones making a crude sculpture. More than anything, Alvin wanted to hightail it out of Piney Grove before its ubiquitous dust took permanent hold in his teeth, his eyes, his mouth. Before memory overwhelmed him.

A car engine burbled. The *ahooga* of a horn. The Ford Model A pulled up slow then stopped. Car was old and a low-end roadster; they must not pay loan officers at Pike County Bank and Trust as much as he'd thought.

A man climbed out of the car. Big guy, overweight. Powder blue shirt, no jacket, no tie.

Alvin figured Roy would be peering out at them from behind the boards that crisscrossed the kitchen window. Unable to go inside to greet his father, Alvin turned back to the man who was now clambering toward him like he owned the place. Which, of course, he did. Or rather, the bank he worked for did.

Alvin licked his dry lips and bent down to grab the handle of his suitcase. Its sides bulged; there should be enough money in the suitcase to get the farm out of foreclosure.

The man had reached him now.

"Long time since you been 'round here, Alvin," the big man said, and Alvin squinted, trying to place the face.

"Eugene Newcomb." Sweat splotched his shirt. "Shame having to meet up again this way," the man said.

No way in hell would Alvin turn the money he'd stolen from Owney over to this bastard.

Just then Roy stepped out of the house, the stubs of his arms hanging incomplete at his sides. No prostheses.

"Where's the rest of you?" Alvin asked in a voice he didn't recognize. Tough guy voice. He hoped no one else could hear the thread of fear beneath it.

"Good to see you, too, son."

Alvin closed his eyes at the sound of his father's voice. When he opened them he saw the rough scars that still rippled across the uneven surfaces of his father's stumps.

"Gonna need you to sign some papers, Roy," Eugene shouted. "Might need to go back inside and get one of yer claws."

"I ain't deaf," Roy said.

"They want to evict you, Pa," Alvin said then. "I've got some money here, Eugene," he said, stalling for time. "How much exactly are we talking about?"

He didn't know why he'd taken the money, an extra duffel bag from the payment due the bootleggers. He didn't even know why he'd come back to Piney Grove.

The fat man swiped his forehead; the cotton came back dark with sweat.

"Oh, no need to go into that, Alvin," he said. "We're far past that point."

"How much?" Alvin asked, his eyes still locked on Roy's. He was trying to get his father to show some weakness, or gratitude, anything. But there was nothing.

"Long time since I seen you, too, Eugene Newcomb. What in hell got into you that day?" Roy asked.

"What you mean?" The fat man's face was already wet with sweat again.

"What you mean, *sir?*" Roy said.

The old man still had dignity; Alvin gave him credit for that.

"I asked what got into you that day of my accident?" Roy said.

Eugene's face reddened.

"Pa, that was a long time ago," Alvin said, impatient at this unexpected turn. "Doesn't matter anymore."

"Oh, it matters," Roy said. "To me it was like it was yesterday. Accident like that—it's a branding iron on your soul."

Roy stepped close to Eugene, who jumped back, scared. Like that rabbit he'd shot, Alvin thought, before he did his death somersault. He could feel the weight of the Colt gun inside his jacket.

"Sometimes," Roy said, "I'd swear it feels like I still got hands. Sometimes my hands get cold, even when the rest of me is hot. Day like today, for instance."

Roy rested a stump on Eugene's shoulder.

"Stop it," Eugene said.

Alvin could feel what Eugene must be feeling: the weight of that stub, so wrong and terrible.

"Just stop it." Eugene turned his back to them and walked as quickly as a big man could back to his car. A dust devil blew up on the road behind him.

"Gonna need your signature, old man," he shouted over his shoulder.

Alvin wondered what Owney would do in this situation and amazingly, laughed. He hadn't laughed in years. And Owney wouldn't laugh when he found out what Alvin had done. But if he were here now, in Alvin's place, the gangster would be swift, reaching under his jacket for the Colt, shooting the loan officer.

"Cat got your tongue?" Eugene had walked back to them, carrying a black valise with gold clasps. He opened this with a loud click and pulled out a folder stuffed with papers. He went through these slowly, licking his index finger to turn each page.

"Here they are," he said finally and thrust a stack of papers in front of Alvin. "Glad you're here since I'm only now recalling that your Pa couldn't have signed this if he'd wanted to!" He guffawed.

"What'll it take to slow this down?" Alvin asked, pushing the suitcase in Eugene's direction with the toe of his shoe. He glanced down at it meaningfully, the way Owney might do.

Eugene licked his lips, and Alvin saw a flicker of the wild boy he'd been. Anything for a dare.

Eugene stuck his thumbs inside the thin belt holding up his pants. "Reckon I'll have to talk to my superiors about that," he said slowly. "But today, sumpin's gotta happen. Your old man has to get out of here. Hell, this place ain't safe for human habitation anyway."

Alvin looked toward the house, the gingham curtains his mother had sewn faded in the window.

"Sign this for your Pa, Parsons, and let's all get out of here. I'm sure you've got better places to be."

No, I don't, Alvin thought. Owney would have figured the theft out by now.

The words on the papers blurred in front of Alvin's eyes.

"Don't sign nothin'," Roy said. "Don't trust any of the Newcombs. You know that well as I."

He was right, Alvin thought. Those supposedly fine, upstanding folks the Newcombs—father a doctor, son an officer at the bank—were as crooked as Owney Madden, Alvin realized. Doc Newcomb had been sent to jail once for embezzling funds. And there'd long been questions about the way he got his patients.

Accidents.

"You and your Pa had a good thing goin' there, didn't you, Eugene?" Roy spit, missing the suitcase by an inch. "My question always was: Did he rope you into it or did you decide to do it all by your lonesome?"

"I don't know what in hell's name you're talking about, old man." Eugene was puffing hard, and his shoes, shiny when he'd first gotten out of the car, were coated with dust.

Roy grinned at him.

Then Alvin remembered: the reins on Eugene's lap, the sharp words his father had said to the boy minutes before the horse reared.

Alvin rubbed the pad of his thumb on the hard grip of the Colt.

"Eugene," he said.

When he turned, Alvin already had the little gun out and was pointing it at Eugene's sweaty forehead.

"Now what you going to do a stupid thing like that for?" Eugene asked. His voice squirmy.

"No need for that, son," Roy said. When Alvin didn't answer, Roy repeated, "No need."

The folder had fallen from Eugene's hand, sending papers flying.

"Put the gun down," Eugene said. "We'll work something out."

He should have warned his Pa about what a troublemaker Eugene was all those years ago, Alvin thought. Should have grabbed the reins of the horse. Should have understood his father's struggle. So many things he should have done; their weight made it hard to breathe.

Maybe if there'd been brothers, uncles, cousins to help out, he'd have stayed. Done his share to keep the farm going. But there'd never been anybody else, just the three of them. After the accident, they'd sit at the table in silence, none of them talking. He knew his parents loved him; he knew they did. But after the accident, something changed. His Pa seemed uninterested in him, focused only on how to use his hooks. Accumulating basic skills like gamblers at the Southern Club accumulated casino chips.

Idle hands are the devil's playground, Roy had said when Alvin was a boy.

Eugene came up close and knocked the gun from Alvin's hand.

"My work here's done," Eugene said. His voice had found its grown-up timbre again.

He kicked the rattan suitcase so it fell over in the dirt.

"I'm going to see that you and your pa here are sent out of town on a hanging rail. Hell, I'll get you put in jail for threatening my life," Eugene said as he headed to the car. "You've made a real mess of things now, Alvin Parsons. Foreclosure's going to be the least of your worries."

"I figure I'm gonna stay around these parts for a bit, Eugene," Alvin said. The sun had sunk a little in the sky, and that meant the day would get cooler. Hell, it was probably cooler inside the dark shadowy rooms of the house.

Roy turned toward the house, and Alvin followed him after picking up the gun from the road.

Inside, he went first to the window above the sink where his Mama stood so often; the glass was long gone and the opening covered by thin plastic and two crossed boards. He watched Eugene drive away. Then he turned to the old kitchen table and ran his fingers along one edge.

Two prostheses lay atop the scarred oak. He remembered the smell of the leather, the way he'd watched his father rub liniment oil to keep it from hardening and cracking. Orangish rust streaked the metal of the split hooks. He felt the gun in his waistband, pulled it out and threw it down on the table. He and Roy were a pair. Hand-less. Gut-less. Wounded, both of 'em.

"Everybody's missing somethin', aren't they?" Alvin said.

"'Suppose so," Roy said. "At least my losses are visible."

Alvin exhaled loudly. "I'm here now, Pa."

"I see that."

"What do you need me to do?"

"Just be here." Roy walked to the sink and used his elbow to light the stove under a long-handled pot.

Alvin wanted to be able to smile but couldn't.

Through the window he heard the hollow chime of cow bones clattering in a gust of wind. In a few minutes, he went to pick up the pot from the stove, so lost in thought he burnt his hand. It hurt like hell, but somebody had to do it.

"Spring Tryout" by Thomas Hart Benton

SPRING, 1933

Missouri, 1933

The boy rode a dark horse, crossing a field of Yellow Stargrass and olive green shadows. A slip of a stream, logs so recently cut their ends were white and circled with clear, brown rings. One had the stump of a broken branch on its side. The dark horse's ears pointed towards a gray farmhouse to the east, and to the left of that, low stalls and three spreading cherry trees blooming pink. On the side of the house a single dark window opened like an unseeing eye. Behind it someone dreamed.

The boy's name was Tom. The pants of his overalls rode high above his brown boots. He rode bareback. The sleeves of his soft, collarless blue shirt were rolled at the elbows. His long fingers wrapped tight around thin reins that stretched taut from the bridle. His hair was brown like the horse, his mouth open like the horse. His hair flew out behind him in the same direction as the horse's tail.

His straw hat hung in the air above the horse's rear, as though a second rider sat beneath it. But that second rider, Ned, lay in a ditch the shape of the horse's shadow. Ned's blue overalls hitched high above his boots, one leg in the air from the fall. Even though he was sitting on his rear in the ditch, it was easy to tell he was the shorter and the younger of the two.

The sky was mostly cloud, with cornflower blue showing through in unremarkable shapes. Last spring, Tom and Ned sometimes ran out of the gray farmhouse and lay on their backs in a soft spot of grass and looked up at the sky. Seeing winged angels and a puppy and once, the Gulf of Mexico.

The horse headed quickly home. Something had spooked the animal; he ran fast.

Inside the gray farmhouse, inside their mother's dream, there were drops of blood on the whitewashed walls of a bedroom. On a nubby white chenille bedspread and pale pink sheets.

Through the single window on the wall, a scene pretty as a picture showed creamy whipped clouds and blue sky, the tops of pink-feathered trees, sweet and silky, dancing in an unseen wind.

In her dream, she stood at the side of the bed. Her arms hung heavy at her sides; one hand clasped the handle of an object so heavy it pulled her whole being down to the floorboards she had varnished on hands and knees one week before. One drop of blood beaded on a wide pine plank; with the round toe of her black shoe, Amber rubbed at it until it disappeared. The floor was clean again now but not the walls or the bedspread or the sheets. Or what lay on the bed in front of her. The thing she would do anything in her power not to see, even as she struggled to wake.

She'd been planning to go into town for groceries today, to take Tom and Ned and let them each get a piece of penny candy, even though she'd have to listen to Mr. Sauger reminded her, loud enough for everyone in the store to hear, that she and Samuel owed $22.75 that better get paid.

There was laundry to wash, Samuel's and the boys', as well as her own. A ham to start. She'd promised a meat and spaghetti pie to her neighbor Inez, might as well make two and save one for dinner. At least that's what she'd been thinking last night when she lay down in bed.

She'd been thankful to have a bed; a mile down the road, Inez and her husband, James, must have slept on blankets on the floor. There'd been a small fire in their house yesterday afternoon. She and Inez and James had been friends since they were children. It was her husband Samuel who was the newcomer, though he hadn't come into their midst until James had left and Amber thought he had left for good.

When Inez and James came up to the gray farmhouse last night to tell Amber the news, she invited them to stay for dinner. She'd stood by the sink pulling out the insides of a chicken, listening to Inez sob and tell her story of how she and James had come home from work to find smoke pouring out the upstairs window. And their bed in flames.

Amber kept her mind busy thinking about dinner; she had potatoes in the pantry and some of last summer's corn in the Deepfreeze.

Through the door to the living room, she could see one leg of James' pressed black pants, one shiny leather shoe. The boys sat on the floor in front of him, like they were in school. She couldn't hear the words he was saying, but she understood the rhythm. He was trying to answer their questions when he had no answers. Eventually, James turned the dial on the radio so the boys could listen.

"I'm glad you were out of the house," she said to him when they finally sat down to eat, having grown tired of waiting for Samuel. She passed the platter of fried chicken, first to Inez then James and then the boys. She'd soaked the chicken in buttermilk, double-dipped it in flour. All the time stealing glances at the screen door, hoping Samuel wouldn't push through it.

Ned made a crater in his mashed potatoes with the back of his spoon and filled it with gravy.

"I'm glad James was with me," Inez sniffled. The tip of her nose was pink from crying, and the flesh on her upper arms jiggled. Amber was afraid she would start to sob again, but Inez took another bite of corn and said, "I wouldn't have known what to do if I'd come home and found that all by myself. Why, James ran right up there and started throwing blankets on top of the fire." She plucked at a button on the front of her green gingham dress.

"Worse part was seeing that smoke," James said. "Could have been a lot worse for all I knew. But it wasn't even that big a fire." He was still handsome nearing 50, and the lines of the boy he'd been still shone in his face. His fingers were long, nails trimmed neat. His white shirt had soot on the arms and front, but except for that, he looked just like the scholar he was.

"At first I thought the fire was coming from your place, Amber." His eyes held hers.

It was Amber's birthday. She had bought herself a layer cake with hard pink frosting and a red candy rose; it sat on a doily-covered plate on the green Formica counter.

"Amber," James said softly. "You feeling all right?"

Amber felt her cheeks go warm and looked down at the cloth napkin in her lap. "Oh my goodness," she said. "Look here." She held up the napkin with its dribble of gravy as though she expected them to tell her what it meant. "I've got to wash this out before it's too late." Her mama had always said, "No matter how poor you are or how bad things are, you can always stay clean."

Inez had his hand on top of James'. "Who would have done such a thing?" she was asking, over and over.

Samuel didn't get home until after ten, after Jzmes and Inez had left. Amber sat across the table from him while he ate, not speaking. She smelled whiskey on his breath.

"Inez shouldn't of been off workin' like that anyway," Samuel said, as though he were answering some question she hadn't had the heart to ask. His fork, piled with mashed potatoes, stopped halfway to his mouth. "She's got a home to run. A husband."

She let him rant awhile. It had been three weeks since he lost his last job, bagging clothes at the cleaners.

Amber was tired but wanted to sit with him, make sure nothing bad happened. When he finally climbed the stairs, she followed him. He went into the boys' bedroom. It was dark and Amber could barely make out the shapes of Tom and Ned under the quilts she'd sewn. Even the quilts were dark and colorless. She said, "Don't do that,' but Samuel sat down heavy next to Ned, her baby even though he was 13, and woke him.

"Didn't do your chores tonight, boy, did you?" Samuel's voice was whiskey-coated, low and somber. For a minute, Amber thought he might just talk awhile then let the boy go back to sleep. In the other twin bed, Tom turned over in his sleep, shifting the quilt so one bare shoulder shone in the moonlight.

"Didn't think I'd know, did you?" Samuel wiped a corner of his mouth with the side of his hand. "But I know. I stopped in the barn. Nobody had mucked the stalls. Nobody did any milkin'."

"No, sir," Ned whispered.

"It's all right, Samuel," Amber said, whispering too. "Inez and James were here. The boys..."

Samuel turned to look at her. His face, and the whole room, seemed to be covered in the same black soot that had soiled James' shirt. All she could see was Samuel's eyes, and there was a sadness in them bigger than anything she'd seen from him during these horrible weeks.

He grabbed Ned's arm, lifting him out of the bed.

"What's going on?" Tom mumbled. "You okay, Ned?"

But Ned wasn't big enough to fend off his father, and Amber knew that's why Samuel had chosen the younger boy. She stood up with them and held on to the crook of Samuel's arm. Her black shoes lifted completely off the floor and she swung in the air. All the while Samuel was shaking Ned's shoulders, saying things like, "You've got to goddamn help your mother and me," and, "That goddamn teacher of yours." Tom had gotten out of bed and was trying to pull his father off Ned, too. Finally, Samuel just let go, turned and walked out of the room, head in his hands.

Amber put her finger to her lips to silence the boys, then quickly followed Samuel into their room. She helped him take off his boots, pants, and shirt, and get under the white chenille spread. When he started to snore, she went back and sat with Ned until he fell asleep with his head in her lap, whule she fingered his brown hair.

She said to Tom, "It'll be all right. You'll clean out the stalls tomorrow. It's Saturday. After you do your chores, you'll get the horse out. It's warm enough now. He'll be ready for that first spring ride."

When both boys had gone back to sleep, Amber went downstairs to the kitchen. With tears running down her cheeks, she scraped the food off Samuel's plate into the barrel out back – the white streaks of potato and bits of glistening skin from the chicken, nuggets of yellow corn, handpicked last August.

Of course now, at the very beginning of springtime, corn was no more than an idea. That's another thing she'd have to do in town— ask Mr. Sauger for more credit so she could buy the seed, full-season hybrid. She'd get it in early this year, she told herself. Almanac said there wasn't much chance of getting mudded in.

The corn would grow fast, like it did every year—"knee high by the Fourth of July," that's what youngsters sang. They'd been so beautiful, her boys. They still were, but something had broken in them just like it had broken in her.

Life sure hadn't turned out the way she'd expected. She could remember days on this farm when she was a girl, watching her mama cook and clean in this very kitchen. Running outside, looking up at the wide sky and all the land around her. Thinking everything was hers for the taking.

On Amber's 16th birthday, she'd climbed one of the cherry trees that dotted the field. The shiny reddish-brown bark peeled and curled. She had on two petticoats, and when James came up beneath her, he reached his hands into the white clouds of them.

Why hadn't they married? She didn't know whose fault that was. It was James and her from the beginning, with Inez, a whole five years younger, running to keep up with them. Sometimes, Amber and James would ride bareback. When Amber and James rode, at just about the age Tom was now, Amber felt the horse beneath her and James in front of her.

When her papa was ready to breed the bay, he'd asked James to come help with the daily tease. "To see if she's in heat," he'd said. Amber had swung back and forth on the gate to the stall while James and her papa led the stallion in. For a few days, nothing happened. Then one day, the bay, Confetti, raised her tail when the stallion came close, her hind legs spread, and peed.

"Look here," Amber's papa said. He was pushing the stallion backwards out of the stall, motioning for Amber to take the lead rope and hold on to the big horse while he showed James what he wanted to show him.

"He called it winking," James told her later in the cherry tree. "The whole little thing just turned right inside out. Your Papa said it meant Confetti was in heat and ready to breed."

It was right after high school when James left. He went to the city, to St. Louis. He didn't say he was coming back. He'd gotten into college. He'd shown Amber the letter with the black seal that looked like the markings on a knight's shield. She wasn't going to college; there wasn't enough money, and her parents needed her help on the farm.

James wrote letters for a while, long ones with stories about what he was learning. Sometimes he'd say he missed her. But it wasn't enough. As a grown woman, Amber tried to figure out if it had been her lack of trust or his lack of love that made things happen the way they happened.

After her parents died in a car crash, Amber moved in with Inez's family down the road. She worked hard for the privilege—doing laundry, washing dishes, beating down the rugs on the steps of the front porch. She lived there for one whole year while they waited for the farm to sell. When it did, it was to Samuel. He didn't look like anybody from around these parts, with his olive skin and dark hair. He had no family of his own, just some money and a strong desire to try to earn his living on the land.

He was tall, like James. He didn't smile too often, but he looked good when he did, and when he bent down to kiss her, he smelled like teas and spices, something that made Amber think of far-away places. Sometimes his brow knitted together in one line of fury, but Amber thought that would go away. She could keep the farmhouse now, and her fields. Pretty soon, her first baby, Tom, came with his beautiful brown eyes and tiny fingers. Seven months before James returned, she gave birth to Ned.

She thought she knew how to be a mother, but other than James, she hadn't spent much time around boys, and her boys weren't like James. They were rougher around the edges, like Samuel. She'd hear them swear when they thought she wasn't listening, words they picked up from their father. They were good boys, did all right in school and were generally respectful. But she always felt she had to stay alert, always felt there was trouble coming just around the corner. The older they got, the more Samuel took to yelling at them. Beating their bottoms with a belt if they talked back.

Some mornings she'd look out the window of her bedroom, past the dark trunks of the cherry trees, and wish the boys had grown up on this farm the way she did. In peace. She was most happy when she caught them having fun, bareback on Confetti's Wonder, or sitting in the dark of the movie theatre, eyes bright and mouths partly open. Just having fun.

There was too much work in this world, she'd decided. She'd worked hard for all her life, and she was tired of it. She was tired of cleaning and cooking and making beds and unmaking them. Tired of laundry and mending old clothes for the boys now that Samuel was out of work. She was tired of watching Samuel drink too much, tired of his rage. He'd hit her once. She got a bruise on her cheekbone that she'd lied about, saying she'd stumbled and hit her face against the saddle rack in the barn. But that wasn't what mattered.

It was hitting the boys that changed things. It was doing what she suspected of him at James and Inez's house. Setting the bed on fire.

Samuel had hated James from the beginning, as though he'd

known something without ever being told about it. He'd mimic the way James talked. "Highfalutin bullshit," he called it. Some nights, when he'd had too much to drink, he'd pull Amber out of bed and make her stand at the window and look across the dark fields. He'd hold her chin in his hand and say, "Look, Amber. See that light down there?" She'd nod yes and hold back any tears that threatened to spill. The light was in James and Inez's bedroom. When Samuel worked the fields for Mr. Brannon, the bank manager in town, he'd come home one night with a small leather case. Inside was a pair of binoculars with a pretty mother-of-pearl inlay. He told Amber he'd found them on a table in the hall when Mrs. Brannon invited him in for lemonade. The table had been filled with objects: a brass magnifying glass, photographs in silver frames, paperweights of all shapes and sizes. "They won't miss the binoculars for one night," he'd said, holding her hand as he led her to the window.

He'd kept his hand on her shoulder while she pretended to focus the lenses. She kept them blurry just the same, making up a whole story about what James was doing to Inez and how a sheet had blown back to reveal one of Inez's breasts. She'd felt Samuel's hand squeeze her shoulder, and then she lay beneath him later that night. She hadn't wanted to make love to him when he drank.

"Where are you, Amber?" he'd shouted as he plunged into her, asking her to be somewhere she couldn't be.

The night of the fire, after she finished cleaning Samuel's plate, she climbed into bed next to him. He had one arm flung high above his head.

She lay quietly in bed, thinking how she should tell the sheriff about the fire. She should tell Inez and James. Samuel was drinking too much these days, everybody in town knew that. He'd lost his job. Lots of people were having hard times now.

But the sheriff and most people in town thought that all in all, Samuel had done quite well by Amber, who'd been alone when her parents died. Hadn't even married until age 29. Amber was quiet; she didn't complain. Not to anybody. Not for all these years.

But she was so tired now, and things had really gone too far. She didn't like that feeling of never being heard, didn't like that feeling of not even hearing herself.

When she'd finished cleaning the dishes and wrapped the leftover chicken, she climbed upstairs and into bed with Samuel. She hadn't even known how angry she was until she lay there listening to him snore, unable to sleep. When the round clock on the nightstand said 11:30, she thought about how in another 30 minutes, her birthday would be over. She had started a new decade. She stayed flat on her back, hardly breathing, staring at the white face of the clock, listening to the quiet tick as the minute hand jumped from one black line to the next.

She got out of bed, climbed back downstairs and held the screen door so it wouldn't slam as she went outside.

She crossed toward the barn. How could she have done things differently? When she was little, she'd talked to the trunks of the cherry trees and heard them talk back. She'd seen light around her parents' faces, light around each blade of Stargrass in the fields. She didn't tell anyone what she saw because she was afraid. The only one she'd ever told was James, and she figured that by now, he must have forgotten. She kept silent about it even when she married Samuel. She'd stepped off Inez's front porch 17 years ago, out of the house where she felt like an outsider, and let herself be lifted up into Samuel's strong arms.

She knew something had to change.

Inside the barn, Confetti's Wonder neighed. She was the only horse left now; when Amber was little all ten stalls had been filled.

She looked for the light around her boys, had seen it in glimpses when they were babies and little ones, but as they grew, she could not see it. She had tried looking for the light around Samuel but could not see it. Whose fault was that? And when she stared at herself in the mirror, a flat, dull portrait stared back.

She found the axe in the barn.

Sometimes in the summer, as a child, Amber would walk out to the cornfield that her father had planted, and her grandfather before him. She'd walk amongst the stalks with her bushel basket and fill it, gripping the ears with her left hand, using the hook to open up the shucks, hands going in opposite directions to clean, and then the quick jerk to break the shank from the stock. She'd toss the freed ear into the basket with the right hand while the left reached for the next one, all in a musical rhythm.

The rough, dry husks scraped her chapped hands and made tiny cuts. At some point she'd put the basket down at her feet. She'd find the maypop, the little white pulps that tasted like citrus and the smell of the corn.

The stalks rose above her head toward the blue sky and the nearing autumn.

Below her was the ground, and the basket of her hard work going up and down the long rows she'd run through as a child, laid down upon it. She'd wipe her palms on her apron, then let them lie quiet and warm on her thighs.

She'd stand without moving. Her eyes would stay open and she was looking and she was seeing, but she wasn't looking for anything, and she wasn't looking at anything. But the stalks were above her and the blue sky above that. The stalks blew in the wind, and pretty soon her breaths would match the wind.

She didn't want to go back home to the gray house where her parents didn't wait for her anymore. Where now there was only Samuel and Tom and Ned, and a darkness from which she wasn't sure she could protect any of them. She didn't want to push through the stalks in the field, to hear the corn scratch against her face and hands. She just wanted to stand without moving. To wait until the blood in her body moved the same way as the wind moved.

In her dream, when she finished the second hack with the axe, she knelt down by the bed, dipped her hands in her husband's blood. She poured it over her right hand and then left, three times on each side. "These hands have committed evil," she said, and cut off her left hand with the axe. She sobbed not knowing how to cut off the other that offended her.

The sound of a horse coming fast to the house woke her from her dream. She heard Ned call to his brother, "Come back and get me! Come back! I fell off!"

Tom laughed and the horse neighed.

The clock said seven. Samuel's head lay on the pillow next to hers, his mouth partly open, pale pink at its edges, dark inside. She could see the rise and fall of his chest under the blanket with its white terry loops, the opening and closing of his nostrils, the soft movement of his eyes beneath their lids. Was he dreaming of her? She had dreamt of him, some horrible thing she couldn't remember in the light of morning.

The day ahead. The grocery. The ham. The spaghetti and meat pie. Yesterday she'd thought about having Inez and James up to the house again for dinner but now she thought, no, remembering James' hand on top of Inez's. She'd make the pie, leave it on the porch while James and Inez were at work.

She should have told Samuel the same things she told James when she sat in the cherry tree. Would it have been different then? Could she have taught him to see the light that wavered around trees, to see God in the pink double flowers of cherry blossoms? Spring, summer, autumn, winter. For so many seasons and years she and Samuel had lived speaking and not speaking. Words had fallen from their mouths like black beetles, day after day. Words that meant nothing yet filled the air between them. Flatbed wagon's broke. Gasoline's up to ten cents. Seeds rotted out. We've got to replant the corn.

Sometimes there were words of love, or what stood for it, spoken at night under clean sheets that had hung on a line between the house and barn. But those were few. More of the nights had the rough music of murmurs and grunts, sounds from deep inside Samuel as he came and tried to bring his light to hers.

The white curtain fluttered at the window. Amber went to look and saw outside her boys and Confetti's Wonder, who was wild and frisky after being cooped up all winter, ready to be let loose for another spring on the farm. She saw Tom's straw hat, its edges curled up, lying on the ground behind the horse. She saw Ned standing up from the ditch, brushing his pants, and beginning to run after Tom, still riding. Both boys had shirts and overalls that would need cleaning but that would have to wait. Just now the horse with its remaining rider was passing two fresh-cut logs, the branch where she'd sat as a girl, tempting a boy and imagining he loved her.

"Edge of Town" by Thomas Hart Benton

UNDER THE WEIGHT OF HIS MOTHER'S BODY

Missouri, 1938

Even before knowing her real name, Arthur hoped she would one day be his wife.

Her real name wasn't Ruby; it was Dorothy Elizabeth McDermott. But she'd taken to wearing lipstick in high school, she'd told him, shaping her lips into a cupid's bow. She carried a push-up tube of Tangee Ruby Rose with her at all times and pulled it from her skirt pocket and applied it slowly, dazzlingly, before Arthur had even learned her name that day in the park in Kansas City.

"Everyone calls me Ruby," she'd finally said. "Everyone except my parents, that is."

"I'm Arthur Trupp," he said as his dog Daisy, named after his mother who'd died in a bizarre accident when Arthur was four, strained against a rope leash. He told Daisy to heel, and to his surprise, the dog obeyed him. Impressed, Ruby batted her eyelashes.

Arthur had only been in the city a week, his first trip away from Laquey. His boss Joe, who had raised Arthur after his mother's death during a tornado, was recuperating in the university hospital after a heart attack. Arthur had come to help care for him, leaving the Esso station, Laquey's only gas pump and Joe's business, closed. People could always drive to Lebanon, Joe reassured him, or even Rolla for that matter.

Arthur fell in love with Ruby just like in the movies, at first sight. She looked like an actress from the silver screen. Pale blue eyes flecked with gold, porcelain skin, and soft blond waves that reminded him both of Jean Harlow and his mother whose early and unexpected death had prevented her from ever growing old.

Beauty. Intrigue. To Arthur's eyes, Dorothy Elizabeth McDermott, Ruby, was a magnet he could not resist. Unlike his overweight mother, whose body had landed on him during the tornado, saving his life, Ruby was thin and willowy.

Thankfully, she took the lead in asking if he'd take her to the movies that weekend. He'd said yes, of course, and yes to every other date she proposed during the next three weeks. He could not believe his good fortune. Arthur Trupp was the happiest he had ever been in his life.

That bubble of happiness was pricked though not completely deflated when Ruby invited Arthur to the large house on Ward Parkway where she lived with her parents.

Ruby's parents and grandparents and great-grandparents were all from Kansas City, so most of the talk that night was about that fine place. They dined on prime rib of beef, green beans with salt pork, a moist corn pudding, and potato rolls. When Arthur said he was only in town for a month, Mrs. McDermott suggested sights he should see: Liberty Memorial. The new Nelson-Atkins Art Gallery.

"That's a luxurious marvel," she said. "And the rose garden and pergola at Loose Park."

"That's where we met, Mother," Ruby said. "I told you."

"Oh yes, dear, I forgot." Mrs. McDermott lifted her lavender cloth napkin to her lip. "Well, back to the new art gallery then." She looked at Arthur. "I think Ruby should work there," she said. "I have a dear friend on the Board of Trustees who tells me he can get her a good placement."

Ruby laughed. Like a bell, a chime, the prettiest sound Arthur had ever heard other than the lullabies his mother had sung to him as a child.

"Nuts to that," Ruby said. She squeezed Arthur's knee under the table.

"So tell us," Mr. McDermott said. "What are you doing here in K.C., Arthur?"

"My boss," Arthur began, "His name is Joe. He's my guardian, actually—he raised me. He had to have an operation. Too important to be done in the small town where he and I live. So I came along to help Joe recover."

The table was silent until Ruby took Arthur's arm and said, "Isn't he the sweetest?"

Mr. McDermott cleared his throat. "Your father…?"

"Gone before I was born," Arthur answered without shame. "It was just my Mama and me. Till she was killed by a tornado that ripped right down the main street of Laquey."

Both McDermotts spoke at the same time.

"Oh my," Mrs. McDermott said.

"And that is…" Mr. McDermott said.

"'Bout 40 miles from Rolla," Arthur said.

Mr. McDermott raised his brows.

"Do you know where Springfield is?" Arthur asked.

Both McDermotts nodded.

"Well, Laquey's about 84 miles if you take 44. And 103 if you take 65."

"You're saying 'Lakeway'?" Mr. McDemott asked. "How's it spelled?"

"L-a-q-u-e-y."

The McDermotts nodded again.

Arthur continued. "There was a Baptist Church there, named after the land of Edom. Like in Isaiah 63." His mother had made certain Arthur knew his Bible, and he could still remember some of the lines: *Who is this that cometh from Edom, in crimson garments?*

"Well then," Mr. McDermott sighed. "I see." He exchanged a glance with Mrs. McDermott at the other end of the table.

"I must see to the dessert," she said and disappeared into the kitchen.

The evening was a disaster: an overwhelming selection of forks and spoons and glasses and a withering glance from Mrs. McDermott when he took a first bite of dessert before the maid had finished setting everyone's plates down. But afterwards, Ruby walked Arthur to the front stoop and pulled him in for a kiss.

Instead of the places Mrs. McDermott had suggested, during the next weeks Ruby took Arthur to jazz clubs, every night after he left Joe's rehab: the Chocolate Bar, the Hi Hat, the Reno Club. She drank gin sours and smoked Lucky Strikes, which she said helped girls stay slim. Arthur loved the jazz, and he loved Ruby, and made love for the first time with her one night in the small room he'd rented near the hospital. Daisy lay on a small rag rug at the foot of the bed.

When it was time to return to Laquey with Joe, Arthur assumed he would never hear from Ruby, but three months later, she wrote to say she was pregnant. She didn't sound unhappy about this. Arthur sat staring at the pale pink stationery with the large DEM monogram and knew his Mama would want him to do the right thing, even if she wouldn't have approved of Ruby's heavy use of makeup.

Despite their horror at the prospect of having Arthur for a son-in-law, the McDermotts insisted on holding a small wedding at their house. Mr. McDermott, who never suggested Arthur call him by his first name—Edgar—took Arthur aside.

"That girl you're marrying…" he said, pointing towards Ruby who stood at an outdoor bar, head back, her hair glowing in the sunlight, cocktail in hand, "…has always had me wrapped around her little finger. Always done what she wanted to do even if the Mrs. and I were dead set against it. I give you a month, maybe two, before she comes running home."

Arthur wished then that he'd insisted on inviting Joe to the wedding so he could have asked for advice on what to say to his new, and clearly unloving, father-in-law. He'd wanted to invite Joe, the only family he had, but that simple request had led to the first fight he and Ruby had, and the first time he'd seen her side with her parents.

Joe hadn't been particularly happy when Arthur told him his plans to marry Ruby. "Don't do it, son. Only met her the once, that day you brought her to see me in rehab. I haven't got a clue what she sees in you. Not a woman your mother would approve of."

Arthur's mother liked humble girls, who didn't drink, wore Peter Pan collars, and had innocent vocabularies. But he hoped once Joe and Ruby got to know each other, all would be well. As his mother used to say, "All will be well and all will be well and all will be exceedingly well." It hadn't been for her, getting killed by that tornado when she was only 40, but Arthur still hoped she was generally right.

He hadn't told Joe that Ruby's drinking and desire to go to jazz clubs most nights worried him, too. But again, once Ruby was away from the presence of her parents, she'd have less to rebel against and could settle down.

To his surprise, she'd agreed to move to Laquey "for a short stretch."

"I want to see where you were born," she said. "This Laquey I've been hearing so much about." She ran one finger down his cheek. "We'll just stay a little while, then come back after this baby's born, won't we, sweetie?"

Joe helped Arthur move Ruby and some of her belongings back

to Laquey. After they had loaded the Chevy 6, Joe stood holding the passenger door open and tipping his blue cap with the black brim and Esso logo in red on white. "At your service, ma'am," he said.

Arthur looked to see if Joe was being sarcastic, but the older man's face gave nothing away.

No one said much on the drive back to Laquey. Arthur filled the car with music from the radio: Orrin Tucker Orchestra, Kay Kyser, Goodman. That evening—it was a Sunday because Joe wanted to be sure to open the gas station first thing Monday morning—they listened to The Chase and Sanborn Hour, with Edgar Bergen and his puppet Charlie McCarthy.

"Broadcasting from Sunset and Vine," the announcer said. "And I've got to tell you there's a standing room only crowd here tonight."

Ruby bounced in her seat, clapping her hands. "Ooooh, I want to get there one day, Arthur. Will you take me?"

Joe cleared his throat loudly and looked out the window while Arthur remained silent.

Those first weeks in Laquey, Ruby's belly grew like a waxing moon. When Arthur's beautiful new wife first arrived in town, everyone made a fuss over her, painting a tiny room above the gas station white and knitting little baby socks. The town still held promise, and business was good at Joe's station.

The McDermotts insisted Ruby come to a hospital in Kansas City for the birth though several Laquey women had offered to help her at home. Arthur objected, but as usual Ruby did what she wanted. She took the train to Kansas City and returned a week later with her and Arthur's son. She named him Thaddeus, after a jazz trumpet player she knew.

When Arthur asked her about the experience of giving birth, partly because he wanted to know what his own mother had gone through giving birth to him, she said she couldn't recall a single pain. Twilight sleep, Joe said. "Makes 'em so happy they forget the pain they have."

Ruby continued to glow the first months after Thaddeus' birth. They moved into an apartment on the second floor of a house on

Conover Lane. Ruby's parents shipped pieces of furniture to them on Ruby's return to Laquey, and Ruby occasionally took the train back to Kansas City to shop for curtains and linens and dishes with her mother. She always took the baby with her.

In between those trips to the city, Mrs. McDermott mailed them postcards of exhibits at the Nelson Gallery: James Abbott McNeill's "Arrangement in Gray and Black," Caravaggio's "St. John the Baptist in the Wilderness," and Asian art that had been collected by Mrs. McDermott's friend.

"Convince Arthur to bring you back," was written on the back of one of these cards. "Surely there are businesses and stores that would hire him."

Arthur had been perfectly satisfied to help Joe out at the gas station all these years. He had no grand ambitions. Winning Ruby's love was as grand a prize as he would get in this lifetime, he assumed. He still considered it a puzzling fluke of good fortune that Ruby had so quickly, and surprisingly, become his wife. She seemed to get pleasure from choosing someone so unlike her parents.

Arthur didn't see much need for accumulating money. He didn't crave fame or fortune, and, at least at first, this didn't seem to bother Ruby. Her parents bought her everything she wanted.

"I need to help old Joe," Arthur explained to Ruby whenever she suggested, now that the baby was here, the three of them move back to Kansas City and leave what she called "boring old Laquey" behind.

But Laquey wasn't boring to Arthur. When he was four, a tornado had indeed ripped through the town. He and his mother had been shopping at Grady's Emporium. She needed new silk hose, she said, and reassured him that they'd be home before the storm broke. It was raining, and there was thunder in the distance. When the firehouse alarm went off, Grady himself told them to come down to the store's cellar.

"But I want to go home," Arthur said, and his mother squeezed his hand and pulled him outside into the driving rain and strong winds. Later, Joe would tell him that no mother would let her child make a decision that large. That Arthur's mother must have had her own reasons for going outside. As they hurried back to their car, a turquoise Ford Tudor, they leaned precipitously into the winds. Arthur saw the car lift up from the street, fly through the air toward him and his mother. It was hours before he was found, still breathing, under the weight of her body. Joe, who ran the local gas station and had come to Sunday dinners at Arthur's and his mother's house for years, took him in and raised him as his own.

"So I owe him," Arthur told Ruby.

The year after Thaddeus was born, Ruby had grown angry as well as bored, and Joe developed asthma.

"Soon as he's well," Arthur promised Ruby, "we'll go back to Kansas City. Or wherever you want to go. Sunset and Vine, if you like!"

She didn't laugh.

Old Joe's health deteriorated. Mid-morning, his coughing would be nonstop. He'd finger a white, red, and gold pack of Old Golds, frown, and then turn to a green tin of Dr. R. Schiffmann's Asthmador Cigarettes, filled with stramonium and belladonna.

Joe would smoke one of these as he sat on the rocker on the small porch of the station. He'd often stay there the rest of the day, watching cars speed by on highway 40 or pull off the dirt road that led to his single Esso gas pump. "Don't know what I'd do without you," he'd say, at least once a day.

"Let me get this one," Arthur would say whenever the next motor car pulled up.

And there had always been a next one. It might be a Buick or Cadillac, an Auburn or a Chevy. A car would pull up every twenty minutes or so, on its way to or from Waynesville or Sedalia or even Kansas City. Folks dressed in work clothes on the weekdays and church clothes on Sunday. Parents with kids in the back seat. Farmers in overalls, a year-round tan coloring the arm that jutted out the driver's window.

"What'll it be?" Arthur would ask. And he'd shoot the breeze about the outcome of the latest Soapbox Derby, or Biddy Crawford's visit to her ailing mother, or the filming of the new movie about Jesse James going on over in Pineville.

Arthur knew hindsight could be merciless. By the time Thaddeus turned two, Arthur realized it might have been better if Ruby had never left Kansas City. She raised Thaddeus and kept house but rarely smiled except when an envelope arrived from her parents. With the money they regularly sent, she bought new shades of lipstick or once, a membership in the Victor Record Society and the free record player that came with it.

Their marriage wasn't perfect, but Arthur figured little was in life. He was happy to have a wife, a son, a home. Sometimes at night, while Thaddeus slept, he and Ruby would slow dance in the living room, she in her stockinged feet and slightly drunk on whiskey, he with his nose buried in her neck, which smelled of Tigress perfume. He'd bought the bottle for her at Christmas, its stopper designed in fake tiger fur.

The morning after Thaddeus turned four, Arthur went to work as usual at six a. m. to open up the gas station. As he fed Daisy, he heard old Joe moving about his small living quarters at the back of the station. When Joe finally appeared on the porch, he was pale and sweaty, his lips blue. Arthur helped him into the rocker and went inside to call a doctor, but when he came back out to the porch, Joe had passed away.

Arthur went back inside and called the undertaker, a man named Holden, to come out to the station to prepare the body. A coffin was built of heart cypress lumber, and a wake was scheduled for the next day at the Coronado, a small hotel just across the road from the station.

Everyone in Laquey attended. Ruby wore a black crinkle fabric dress with a wide silver belt. She'd dressed Thaddeus in a small brown suit her parents had sent for him to wear at church on Easter. People milled about, enjoying molasses drop cookies and grapefruit fizz punch Mrs. Holden had provided. Arthur sat quietly at the foot of the closed coffin, thinking about death, about how it had felt lying under his mother's body. From where he lay on the sidewalk, he had seen that the store he and his mother had just run out of was no more. Gone, like that.

Mr. Holden, who was also Laquey's part-time mayor, asked for everyone's attention. "All of us know what a blessing Arthur Trupp was to our dear Joe," he began.

Arthur looked to Ruby, who sat with Thaddeus on her lap near the back wall.

Mr Holden grabbed Arthur's elbow and pulled him into the center of the small crowd.

"Joe thought as highly of you as I do, Arthur. I know he wanted to thank you for all you did for him these last years."

"There's no—" Arthur began, but Mr Holden raised his hand to silence him.

"Joe's left the gas station to you."

Arthur heard Ruby cry out, "No!"

"I—" he began.

But Mr. Holden interrupted him. "The station is yours." He lifted a cup of punch high in the air. "I know you'll continue to do Joe—and Laquey—proud."

Arthur had never been good at thinking fast on his feet, but he tried hard now. He could sell the station, he thought, staring at Ruby and trying to convey that possibility to her through his eyes, which he'd opened wide. They could sell it, he thought and tried to silently say to Ruby across the room, take the money to K.C. and get a small house. Not too close to the McDermotts.

But she refused to meet his eyes. He released the hope of communicating with her across thin air and scanned the faces of the people around him. Some congratulatory, more downcast. Since the highway had been realigned that fall, it no longer went straight through Laquey. Everyone there knew how few cars pulled off for gas anymore and how fewer still bought a cold drink at Parsons' store or spent the night at this Coronado hotel. What they did know was that their town no longer had a future.

Arthur also knew that if these people he'd spent all but one month of his life with lost one more thing, if they lost the simple presence of Joe's Esso station, something in them might die, too.

So he cleared his throat. "Thank you. I'll fill your gas tanks and wash your cars and clean your engines the best I know how. All in Joe's good memory."

There was a smattering of applause, and Mr. Holden wrapped his arm around Arthur's shoulders.

Ruby didn't speak to Arthur that night or the next morning when he kissed her before going to work. He closed the station early and went home mid-afternoon. He found Mrs. Holden there, with Thaddeus asleep in her lap. Ruby had left a note.

"I'll be back for Thaddeus," it read.

She'd been gone for a week now. Every day after work or what there was of it, Arthur took Thaddeus with him to the Esso station and waited for the 5:15 train from Kansas City. He tried to distract the boy by throwing a stick for Daisy to fetch.

But Thaddeus kept asking, "Where's Mama?"

At first, Arthur answered him patiently. "Mama took a trip, sweet boy. She'll be back to us real soon."

On Friday, Arthur and his son stood at the bend in the dirt road. They watched the steam locomotive pull eight cars behind it, watched its wheels turn in unison, watched the thick black smoke pulse out of the smokestack. Arthur waited for the train to slow down, to stop its rolling wheels, but it did not. Thaddeus let his arms fall to his side before Arthur did.

Then, together, they walked back to the station, Thaddeus scuffing his canvas shoes in the dirt road and Arthur with head bowed.

A paper cup rolled down the steps of the empty Coronado Hotel. Thaddeus reached for Arthur's hand.

Arthur looked down at his son, who, he realized with a start, was the same age Arthur had been when he lost his mother. He remembered how often she had read the Bible verse about Edom to him. Isaiah 63. "It's a lonely passage," she'd said. "But a glorious example of how even in the lowest places we can praise the Lord."

By now he knew what she had meant. He wondered what he should tell the boy, and if he could summon the courage he knew he would need.

AFTERWORD

One day, considering what to write next, I sat staring at an early edition print by Thomas Hart Benton hanging on my office wall. I'd been writing short stories for many years, some triggered by events in my own life. But I wanted to see beyond the limits of my own "story," to write something less autobiographical in origin.

My original intent was to transport my imagination to a time and place radically different than my own. To escape the constraints of my own life experiences. Over the next years, I accomplished this, relishing the research I did for short stories based on nine of Benton's black-and-white lithographs, all set in Missouri and Arkansas in the 1930s and 40s.

In the idyllic scene portrayed in Benton's "Spring Tryout," the print hanging on my wall, a horse galloped across a field. One boy in overalls sat astride its back and a second seemed to have just fallen off in the moment the artist had captured. In the distance, pink blossoms feathered trees near a gray farmhouse.

That first day, I began the new story simply by describing what I saw in the picture:

The boy rode a dark horse, crossing a field of yellow stargrass and olive green shadows. A slip of a stream, with logs nearby so recently cut their ends were white and circled with clear, brown rings. The horse's ears pointed toward a gray farmhouse to the east, and to the left of that, low stalls and three spreading cherry trees blooming pink. On the side of the house a single window opened like an unseeing eye.

I was drawn to that small gray farmhouse in the distance, curious how it might be part of the boy's life:

On the side of the house a single window opened like an unseeing eye. Behind it the boy's mother dreamed.

The next stories I wrote mirrored this pattern of creation. I found an old book of Benton's black and white lithographs. One by one, I chose a picture that engaged me. I began imagining lives for the people Benton had portrayed: Two women standing by a flooded river, looking at submerged houses and trees. A black fiddler sitting on a stool while a white couple and several women dance. A well-dressed man standing near the white carcass of a cow, suitcase dropped on the dirt road behind him, stroking his beard as he looks at a boarded-up shack. A man and a boy standing near an old gas station with a single pump, raising their arms as a train rolls past in the distance. A mother embracing her son, in military uniform, as another train approaches.

On a recent trip to visit Benton's museum in Kansas City, Missouri, I learned that during the summers, the artist often took long walking journeys across the country. On these trips, he sketched the ordinary Americans he saw: coal miners, steelworkers, loggers, field hands and farm wives.

Benton memorialized these ordinary people in his art, in a way few American painters had. Then I, as fiction writer, used their visual representations as starting points for my own creative journeys.

One by one the Americans memorialized by Benton took on new life in my imagination. The stories I made up for them were realistic as far as historical detail for the setting. But their personal lives were created from whole cloth, fabricated by me.

As I researched, I read about county fairs and Esso gas pumps, model B Fords and victory gardens. travelling preachers and gangsters like Owney Madden and Lucky Luciano who made Hot Springs, Arkansas, their summer home. Fels Naptha soap used for everything from cleaning windowsills to treating poison ivy to attempts to wipe out stains that ran through family lineages.

As so often happens, research often led serendipitously to

story lines. I learned that men could commit their wives to mental hospitals simply because the women were sad after a miscarriage or tired of doing their chores. I learned about a town particularly hard hit during the Great Flood of 1937 where a church straddled not only county but state lines:

Half the church's thirty benches of hand-hewn sycamore were in one state and half in the other, enabling the members of the congregation to walk up the aisle on their side of the church and attend services without ever stepping into the other state. Come Sundays, folks would file in, lean their guns against the wall, and sit down in the pews on their designated side.

So as I read, the two-dimensional painted figures took on lives far beyond what Benton had intended. I gave them stories: The mysterious woman dancing to fiddle music became a bone setter, descendant of a long line of healers. That boarded up shack puzzling a traveler turned out to be his childhood home.

Despite my initial desire to stop writing semi-autobiographical fiction, despite escaping to times and places radically different than my own, I found parts of my own psyche in these made-up characters. As I wrote, I imagined that these long-dead folks Benton had painted had interior struggles not so different from my own. Marital and parental challenges. Their griefs, their grit, their great loves and losses were, in fact, similar to my own, ¾ of a century later.

 Donna Baier Stein is the author of *The Silver Baron's Wife* (PEN/New England Discovery Award, Bronze winner in Foreword Reviews 2017 Book of the Year Award, more), *Sympathetic People* (Iowa Fiction Award Finalist, Indie-Book Awards Finalist), *Sometimes You Sense the Difference* (poetry), and *Letting Rain Have Its Say* (poetry). She was a Founding Editor of *Bellevue Literary Review* and founded and publishes *Tiferet Journal*. Her work has been published in *Virginia Quarterly Review*, *Writer's Digest*, *Saturday Evening Post*, *New York Quarterly*, *Prairie Schooner*, and many other journals and anthologies.

Acknowledgments

Eight of these stories appeared in different form in the following publications:

"Spring 1933" appeared in *Virginia Quarterly Review*

"Pointing East, Where Things Happen" appeared in *Summerset Review*

"Trouble at the Dance Hall" appeared in *Green Hills Literary Lantern*

"Morning Train" appeared in *Forge* and was nominated for a Pushcart Prize

"Under the Weight of His Mother's Body" appeared in *Free State Review*

"The Sweet Perfume of Somewhere Else" appeared in *St. Ann's Review*

"Prodigal Son" appeared in *Gargoyle*, Summer 2017

"A Landing Called Compromise," *Best Short Stories from the Saturday Evening Post Fiction Contest 2018 Anthology* and runner-up 2018 Saturday Evening Post Fiction Contest

THANKS

I'd like to first thank those who helped with acquiring permissions to reprint the Thomas Hart Benton lithographs in this book: Joyce Faust of Art Resource Inc.; Janet Hicks, Director of Licensing of the Artists Rights Society; and James Kohler, Department Coordinator of Photographic and Digital Imaging Services at The Cleveland Museum of Art.

Thank you to two former high school classmates: Lance Mushung for invaluable help verifying historical detail in the stories, and David Peck and his wife Vicki for taking me to the Thomas Hart Benton Home and Museum in Kansas City, Missouri.

Thanks, too, to the editors who first published these stories in literary journals. I'd like to mention two in particular:

Adam Davis, Editor of *Green Hills Literary Lantern*, who accepted two of the Benton stories for publication and very generously agreed to write the informative preface to this book.

Staige Blackford, the former editor of *Virginia Quarterly Review*, who accepted the first Benton story I wrote, "Spring 1933." I'll never forget the phone call during which Staige said he and his readers hadn't been as excited about a submitted story since the first ones they received from Ann Beattie.

An editor's faith in a writer means a lot.

Thanks are also due to my colleagues in the Two Bridges Writing Group for their careful look at drafts and revisions and to Will Allison, a contributing editor of *One Story*. Will, in particular, provided invaluable editing advice on the full manuscript.

I remain very grateful to Walter Cummins and Thomas E. Kennedy, who have not only written many terrific books themselves but also done so much for other writers by establishing Serving House Books. This is now the third book of mine this traditional small press has published, and each experience has been both exciting and pleasurable.

Gratitude, too, to my students at The Writers Circle and in

the classes I conduct in my home for their own enthusiasm and persistence on the writer's journey.

To my parents for nurturing my love of not only Benton but all things Kansas City and to my grown children, Jon and Sarah, who help balance my dives into the past with their trajectories into the future.

For more information, or if you would like me to speak to your book club or other group in person or via Skype, please email me at donna@donnabaierstein.com. I'd love to hear from you and, like all writers, will appreciate any reviews you leave online.

Thank you to you, the reader.

CREDITS

Hill / Art Resource, NY

"Flood" 1937 lithograph
The Cleveland Museum of Art

"Prodigal Son" 1939 lithograph
Ackland Art Museum, The University of North Carolina at
Chapel Hill / Art Resource, NY

CPSIA information can be obtained
at www.ICGtesting.com
Printed in the USA
FFHW012217150219
50545793-55834FF